# THE SOLACE OF STARS
## A CITY OF SILVER NOVELLA

T. L. MORGAN

# CONTENT WARNINGS

This novella deals with the following topics that may be sensitive to some readers. Please read with care.

- Emotional neglect and abuse by a parent
- Domestic violence
- Suicide (discussions of, and off-page instance)
- Parent death
- Bullying
- (Unintentional) misgendering

# 1

Three misfortunes found Leif Trysz on the first day of the year:

First, they passed out in the washroom.

Then, they broke their mother's favorite bowl.

And then their mother kicked them out.

"*What?*" Leif stared at their mother—the steadfast and over-accommodating apothecary that everyone in the High District loved—and tried to find the real meaning behind her words. Because those words—*You need a reality check, and I need you gone*—were so unfathomable, even coming from a mother as cold and indifferent as her, that Leif could not believe her. "Y-You can't kick me out! Where—"

"Can't I?" Nel planted her hands on her hips. "Last I checked, this was my house—which I bought and fixed and have maintained with *my* hard-earned money from *my* thriving business, and you know quite well that I don't have room for anything that's not useful to me." She stormed to the closet in the kitchen and grabbed a canvas backpack, then flung it at Leif; it landed with a *fwump* at their bare feet. "Pack. You have ten minutes. Master Beldon still owes me a favor, and taking you off my hands will do me more good than any gold he could possibly give me."

Leif was frozen. Master Beldon? What were they supposed to do for *him*? Leif was an apothecary's apprentice, not—not a *doctor*, or anything else a vampire hunter might need.

They stared blankly at the bag on the floor before them, suddenly conscious that they were shivering. An unpleasant sweep of cold seeped down their body, from the back of their neck where their hair gathered in a damp heap, down to their toes on the frigid wood floor. A voice in the back of their mind begged them to defend themself, to stand up to their mother and refuse to let her toss them out like an unwanted object. But that was just it; they *were* unwanted; she'd said it herself. Even being her child wasn't enough anymore.

"Did you hit your head too hard when you lost your wits this morning?" Nel's voice rose to a dangerous volume; Leif had only seen her this angry one other time, and even the memory of it made them shrink back. "That was your own fault, too, you know! If you weren't so damned forgetful, you wouldn't have let the pain get that bad. Now go on, *pack*. You have eight minutes now, and when that time is up, you will be out of this house whether you're ready or not. It's up to you whether you freeze out there." She pointed toward the stairs. "*Go.*"

But Leif's feet were stuck to the floor. "W-

Why?" They hated the stammer in their voice, hated the way they got choked up at even the slightest hint of their mother's anger, whether it was directed at them or not. She'd always scolded them for being overly sensitive, and now they understood why; they must look so pathetic to her —trembling and half-dressed, their hair a wet and tangled mess, their eyes welled with tears.

"*Why?*" She crowed, and Leif knew she was mocking them. "The mere fact that you haven't put the pieces together validates my decision! And no, this isn't about the bowl—I don't give a damn about the bowl, but this is the fourth time *this month* that you've wasted my ingredients by fucking up a recipe or dropping something or other such clumsiness. You are careless and lazy, and those are only two of many reasons why you'll never keep this business afloat. I've always known it, too." She shook her head, lip curling in distaste. "My sister told me to give you a chance, to keep giving you fucking chances, but I'm done. No more. *You're* done. You won't be the reason I lose everything I've fought so hard to gain. No more hiding, no more spacing out in your room, no more slinking by on *my* hard work."

Warm tears slid silently down Leif's cheeks. They'd always known that they didn't meet their mother's expectations for the apothecary business, but they'd thought...Well, clearly their thoughts didn't matter. Clearly *they* didn't matter.

"Don't look at me like that," Nel scoffed. "You're almost eighteen—basically an adult, so act like it. You should be grateful I'm giving you somewhere to go rather than letting you figure it out. There are worse things than being sent to a wealthy family's mansion."

Maybe that was true, but that didn't make this any less of a punishment—one they'd never even thought to fear. Leif suddenly couldn't stand to look at their mother any longer. Clamping a hand over their mouth to muffle a sob, they grabbed the backpack and ran upstairs to gather whatever pieces of their life would fit in one bag.

Beginnings brought challenges, and the start of a new year was no exception. Nor was the start of a new chapter. In Leif's experience, these things came in threes: three misfortunes this morning meant that a trio of positives was in store for them. The universe may be chaotic, but there was a balance to all things, even when those things were in flux. Leif just had to get through the obstacles that lay ahead, and then everything would be fine.

*Everything will be fine.* They repeated the feeble optimism to themself as they came to a stop in front of the gates to the Beldon estate. Their stomach twisted with dread, adding a fresh twinge of discomfort alongside the cramps that had been plaguing them since last night. Nausea roiled through them, but they eased it with a deep breath; the last thing they needed was to faint on the Beldons' doorstep.

Grasping the pendant that was strung around

their neck, they reached out with their free hand and pushed the gate. It opened smoothly and silently, welcoming Leif onto the long path that sliced up the grounds of the sprawling estate. Small, exquisitely manicured holly bushes lined the path, but no trees dared interrupt the swathe of snow-covered yard that spread from the mansion down to the road. A neat cluster of oaks and pines huddled on either side of the lawn, not a root stepping out of line. Leif eyed the massive house with trepidation as they approached the column-framed entrance, and as they drew closer they saw that someone was waiting for them on the steps.

Leif had never seen Marcus Beldon, but they knew this was him. He couldn't be anyone else. Tall and broad-shouldered and splendidly dressed, the master of House Beldon guarded the doors to his home with his chin tipped up and his hands clasped behind his back. His coal-black coat sharpened his silhouette, a stark contrast to the pure white waistcoat that was only slightly visible beneath his shining silk cravat.

Leif forced themself to keep walking despite the nervous spike of their pulse. They felt their face flush under Marcus Beldon's scrutiny, and quickened their pace so as to shorten the awkwardness of being watched. They were suddenly and uncomfortably conscious of how haphazard they appeared: their hair was still loose and uncombed, their clothes were rumpled, their boots were scuffed and their laces untied. They clutched the strap of their backpack and took one last deep breath before coming to a pause at the bottom step of House Beldon.

Marcus's sharp blue eyes pinned them in place. His stony face revealed nothing; if he was perturbed at Leif's presence, they couldn't find a hint of it. His mouth was an expressionless line beneath his graying mustache, and if not for a slight twitch of his eyebrow, Leif might've been staring up at a statue.

"Iris Trysz, I presume?" he said.

"Y-Yes." Out of habit, Leif nearly let the name slide, but something compelled them to say, "But I prefer to be called Leif, sir."

Marcus Beldon inclined his head. "Leif Trysz. Welcome to House Beldon. Please come in, and I'll show you to your lodgings."

Leif blinked, hesitant to move even after Master Beldon turned to stride through the doors—which opened for him with uncanny timing. Were they truly so immediately welcome? That greeting had been...*amicable*. Leif would dare to say even sort of *warm*. And were they to understand that they'd have their own room here?

Anticipation spurred them forward and finally allowed them to trot up the steps and into the house, but their flutter of hope was short-lived. An eerie sense of foreboding greeted them when they entered the foyer; this was not their new home. Their mother would never have flung them at the Beldons if it meant Leif would be welcomed into a life of luxury. This was a punishment, not a glittering opportunity. They'd be lucky if scrubbing the flawless marble floor of this foyer was the worst they got saddled with.

"Your mother told me of your apothecary knowledge," Master Beldon said as he led Leif toward the elegant staircase that faced the front doors. "I understand that you have a mind for herbs, tinctures, and medicines. Is that correct?"

"Yes, sir," Leif replied. They debated for a second if they should elaborate, but then a sharp cramp twisted in their abdomen and chased off any further explanation they might've given. A fresh wave of nausea blurred their vision and made them nearly miss a step. They clenched their teeth, gripped the banister tighter, and pushed themself onward. "Herbal remedies are my specialty," they managed to say, "especially for pain management and stress relief. Mental health is important to me, and I hope to offer a calm, refreshing, and safe space for anyone who needs it. I-If that would benefit anyone in this house—"

"Certainly." Master Beldon glanced over his shoulder as he came to the first landing. "I admit I did not know what I would do with you when your mother insisted I hire you, but my family must be at their very best at all times, and that requires strong presence of mind and the ability to manage stress. Naturally, in our line of work, injuries are common. While we have a physician to handle the worst of it, an extra expert in pain management is never a detriment. I think you will serve us well, Mis— Ah...forgive me, what prefix shall I use?"

"Oh, um..." Leif paused a step beneath him, momentarily panicking. They hadn't considered that they should choose a preferred prefix alongside their name and pronouns. *Miss* certainly wasn't right, but *mister* felt just as wrong. Their mind blanked of all other options. "T-That's not necessary, sir, just Leif is fine."

"Very well. Anyhow..." He led the way up two more flights of stairs, bringing Leif to a long, wide hallway lined with plain brown doors. While the other corridors Leif had passed were elegantly decorated with portraits and tapestries on the walls, this hall was plain: the white walls were unadorned save for three unlit sconces, and the hardwood floor was bare. It was noticeably chillier than on the lower stories.

"Our high-ranking staff live on the third floor, but I'm afraid all of the rooms are occupied," Master Beldon said, striding across the hall. "Given your unexpected arrival, there was not time to prepare a proper room for you, but..." He opened a door that was about a foot shorter than the rest of them. "The attic is free. Have a look."

Leif shuffled toward the door and poked their head in. An iron staircase spiraled up, ending at a landing that jutted out about ten feet above. With a wary glance at Master Beldon, Leif climbed up the steps and found another door at the landing; they pushed it open, and followed three dusty steps into a modestly-sized space with a slanted ceiling and a loft up in the corner to their left.

It was empty. Dusty, dreary, neglected. Leif had no idea how they would make a functional living space out of this room. Where were they supposed to sleep? How would they get a bed up here? Where would they keep their belongings, scarce as they were? They doubted there was a washroom or even the plumbing for one up here, let alone the fixings for a kitchen. Would they have to share those spaces with the Beldon family? Would they even be welcome to?

They realized their hands were shaking and clenched them tight against their chest, taking a deep breath. *Everything will be fine.*

Leif went back down the spiral stairs and bowed their head to Master Beldon. "I can make it work. Thank you, sir. I'm very grateful to you and your family."

"I'll send a maid to bring you a broom." Master Beldon turned to leave. "You'll start your work in three days. I expect you to have a selection of those tinctures readily at hand should I or any of my children need something. In the meantime, acquaint yourself with the family. And if you require anything else, I trust you'll find the appropriate staff."

He left without another word, disappearing down the stairs before Leif could articulate any of the dozens of questions they still had. They hugged their arms around their body and wondered if they'd ever felt so alone.

# 2

LEIF LINGERED there in the attic stairwell until an agonizing cramp dragged them out of their reverie. Pain reeled through their body, twisting deep in their abdomen. They stumbled back against the wall, pressing their hands to their stomach, but the pressure provided little relief. They squeezed their eyes shut and waited for the wave of nausea to pass; their head swam dangerously, and next thing they knew, they were on the floor.

"Damn it," they muttered. Their head fell against the wall at their back, and for several minutes they couldn't move. Even blinking made them dizzy, and the ache in their abdomen dragged all the way down their legs. They longed for their bed and the water pouch they heated up to soothe the cramps, and they mentally kicked themself for letting their pain medicines lapse. In this state, they'd never fall asleep, even with somewhere comfortable to lie, and heat would only do so much.

So there they sat, trembling in delirious agony

in a dim stairwell with nothing but a hard floor to look forward to as their bed.

They hardly noticed the tears welling in their eyes until they fell. This had all happened so quickly; just this morning, they never would have expected to end their day anywhere other than the home they'd always known. No, that home wasn't warm or loving, and no, their mother didn't hesitate to let Leif know that they were just another expense in her ledger, but it was the only home they knew.

But they weren't going back, were they?

"Hello? Is someone up here?"

Leif startled out of their miserable haze and realized too late that someone was approaching the attic door. They dragged themself to their feet, steadying themself on the wall, and stepped into the hallway. A woman of perhaps forty with brilliant green eyes and a mane of brown curls greeted them with a soft smile—a smile which quickly vanished when Leif stepped into the light.

"Gods, are you okay?"

*I look that bad, huh?* Leif gave a weak shrug. "Um..."

"You look like you're about to faint! Come here." The woman hurried to their side and wrapped an arm around them, then ushered them down the stairs, steadying them when they stumbled. When the two of them reached the second floor, she directed them through a doorway into a short hall, and finally through an ornate white door into a cozy room.

"Sit," the woman commanded, and Leif

collapsed into a plush armchair without protest. Their head was spinning again, and their legs felt weakened just from the stairs and the short walk. They felt clammy and cold beneath their sweater, even as the relentless pain twisted an unpleasantly hot ache in their belly.

The woman knelt in front of them and touched the back of her hand to their cheek. "Hmm, you're a little warm. Are you ill? In pain?"

Leif couldn't speak for a moment as another cramp twisted their insides. "Ugh...cramps...bad. S-Sorry, I'll be fine, just..." A groan broke through their gritted teeth.

"Goodness, that bad? Hang on, love, I have just the thing." She darted across the room and then returned promptly with a steaming teacup and a little jar full of orange powder. She sprinkled the powder—turmeric, if Leif had to guess—into the tea, which Leif could already identify as ginger thanks to its aroma. After giving it a stir, she placed the cup in Leif's hands. "Here, drink this. It's ginger tea with a sprinkle of turmeric. An apothecary a few blocks over recommended it to me years ago and I've used it for everything from headaches to stomach aches to menstrual pains. It's a lifesaver during this time of the month."

Oh, Leif knew this remedy very well, and knew precisely the apothecary from which this woman had gotten it. The irony was bitter, but at least they knew it would work. "Thank you," they murmured, and downed the drink in one go.

The woman touched their shoulder again, then went across the room to a cabinet and brought out a small, lumpy pillow. Leif eyed her curiously as she set it in a bowl and placed the bowl in front of the fireplace.

"It's a heat pack," she explained as she took a seat in the chair beside Leif's. "It'll help relax your muscles and release some of the tension that makes the cramps worse. Is it always this bad for you?"

Leif nodded. "Pretty much. Usually I can stay on top of the medicines that lessen the pain, but..." They winced. "Today was chaotic."

"Ah, so my suspicion is correct—you're the apothecary's apprentice?"

"Well..." Leif ducked their head. "I guess I'm not an apprentice anymore, since I'm on my own."

"Fair enough." The woman smiled and pushed her hair behind her ears. "Iris, right?"

Leif hesitated, but they'd already told Master Beldon their preferred name, and there was no going back now. "I— I actually prefer Leif, ma'am."

"Oh! Forgive me. When your mother requested that we hire you, she didn't tell us—"

"She doesn't know," Leif said, then cringed when they realized they'd cut her off. "S-Sorry, I didn't mean to interrupt. But...my mother doesn't know I'd rather be called Leif. She..." They swallowed. "Well, it seemed easier to not further inconvenience her."

"Inconvenience...?" The woman's voice grew soft, and then she fell quiet for a minute. "I have a lot of respect for Nel Trysz and I quite literally owe her my life—and my youngest son's life as well. I'm...shocked to hear that you are perhaps not treated with the same care which she shows her customers."

"No one would believe it," Leif murmured. They'd tried, once, when they were much younger, to tell their aunt that they thought something was wrong—other children they knew loved their mothers, and were showered with affection and attention and comforts—but their aunt had brushed off their feeble attempt to ask for help. *Of course your mother loves you*, Leif was told, but that so-called love was hardly comparable to what Leif *thought* love should look like.

"Her reputation precedes her," they continued. "She's so famously kind and compassionate to everyone else, bending over backwards to find just the right solution to every problem that comes through the door. I swear, half the High District is her best friend. But I guess after helping all of her clients, she has nothing left for me."

The woman gave a short, sharp laugh. She gazed at the flickering fireplace, shaking her head. "Trust me, I understand."

Leif was curious to know how she related to that, but they knew better than to ask. When it was clear that their conversation was done for now, they closed their eyes and leaned their head on the cushion behind them. Dull aches still throbbed in their abdomen, but the pain was far less than it had been even five minutes ago. The nausea had subsided, and in the absence of agony, they were suddenly exhausted.

"Here, love." Leif hadn't heard the woman get up, but she now stood at their side with the heat pack. Leif took it and discovered it was filled with pellets of some sort; they felt too small to be beans, but maybe some kind of grain?

"It's rice," the woman said, clearly reading Leif's curiosity. She laughed softly when their eyebrows shot up. "I know, it seems like a wasteful use of such an expensive grain, but I've had that pillow for...well, probably since I was younger than you, and rice wasn't such a luxury where I grew up." She resumed her seat beside Leif. "That should hold the heat for a good while. Feel free to keep it for the week if you need to. A few minutes right by the fire will get it nice and warm."

Leif placed the pouch on their stomach, sighing in relief as its warmth eased beneath their skin. "Thank you. Ideally I won't need it past tomorrow. The first two days are the worst."

"Oh, don't I know it." The woman smirked. "You rest here as long as you'd like. Did Marcus set you up with a room on the third floor?"

"No, uh...the attic was all that was left."

The woman's eyes widened. Leif didn't think it was possible for a face as soft and kind as hers to show anything close to anger, but her eyes lit up with fury. "He put you in the *attic?*"

"He said the third-floor rooms were all occupied," Leif said. "I don't mind, really. I don't need a lot of space. It's just...well...the attic is empty."

The woman looked affronted—probably as much as Leif ought to have felt. "Oh, *that*..." She scoffed. "That is unacceptable. You deserve a furnished, habitable room, not some dusty corner!

If you're feeling better tomorrow, come with me downtown. I have a few shops to visit, and while we're out, we'll find some proper furniture for you. You can pick it out, and it'll be yours. In the meantime, you are more than welcome to stay here in this parlor and sleep on the daybed. I apologize that it's not ideal, but I assure you it's only temporary. I will be having a *strong* word with my husband about this."

Leif's heart missed a beat. Her *husband?* They supposed they should've guessed it, but knowing that this was the wife of Marcus Beldon made it feel all the more like they were inconveniencing her. They started to get up. "M-Madam Beldon, I'm so sorry, I didn't—"

"Oh, no, no." She shot them a hard look that immediately put them back in their seat. "None of that, now. My husband is the master of this house, not me. Call me Natasha, and please, Leif, be welcome. If there is anything else I can do to make your stay with us more comfortable, please don't hesitate to ask."

Leif already knew they absolutely would hesitate to ask.

Why should they expect special treatment, anyway? They were mortified now that they'd confided those things about their home and their mother to Master Beldon's wife. What if she said something to him, and it got back to Leif's mother? If their honesty affected her reputation, even to one family—to one *person*—Leif had no idea what she'd do to them. She'd already kicked them out. What was worse? Having them exiled from the city? Even if she didn't have that power, surely Marcus Beldon had the right connections to make it happen. Leif didn't think she was that petty, but they also had never thought she'd kick them out.

This was what their mother had always meant when she'd scolded Leif for being too trusting, wasn't it? But if every kind person could just as easily betray them, what use was there in trusting anyone at all?

Nel seemed to navigate this vicious corner of the world with such ease—such comfort, even— and Leif didn't understand the unspoken lines between themself and every other person. Who was a friend? Who was to be believed and followed, and who was to be avoided? How would they know, before it was too late?

"*Mama!*"

Leif startled out of their thoughts at the shrill cry that carried down the hall. Natasha smiled and quietly excused herself, crossing the room to the door.

"In here, love! Why, hello! What are you up to? C'mere, there's someone you should meet."

Natasha came back, now with a child in her arms. The boy couldn't have been more than five or six, and he was nearly the spitting image of his mother. His chubby face was scattered with freckles, and his green eyes gazed at Leif with curiosity. Natasha gently ruffled his curls and kissed his cheek, then set him down. He kept close to her, though, clinging to her side.

"Hi there," Leif said with a wave.

He stared at them a moment longer, then shyly waved back. "Hi."

"What's your name?" Leif asked.

The boy frowned. "What's yours?"

Leif chuckled. "My name is Leif."

"*Leef*," the boy repeated, drawing out the vowels. "I'm Cyrus. What are you doing here?"

"Cyrus, is that polite?" Natasha said.

He looked up at her, then back to Leif. "What're you doing here, please?"

Leif shared an amused look with Natasha. "I'm here to...uh..." How were they supposed to define *apothecary* to a six-year-old?

"Leif is here to help take care of you and Poppy and Joel and Arthur," Natasha explained. "You know how Dr. Adriyen gives you medicine when you don't feel good? Leif is going to do that, too."

Cyrus made a face. "Doctor's medicine is icky."

Leif laughed softly. "Hopefully mine is less icky. I can help if you can't sleep, or if you're sad, or if your tummy hurts, or...if you just want to talk to someone." They smiled. "I'm here to help. To be a friend."

Cyrus blinked a few times, then smiled. "Okay!"

"Where's your sister, Cyrus?" Natasha asked. "I thought you were playing."

He hugged her leg. "She said we were done. And then Arthur came in and told Poppy to follow him to see something, and that I couldn't come. I think they went outside."

Natasha sighed. "All right. You stay here with me, then. Leif is going to stay, too, okay?"

"Okay. Leif can stay."

"How about we play a song for h— Er, forgive me, I don't wish to assume." Natasha looked up at Leif. "How shall I refer to you?"

"Them." Leif flickered a smile.

Natasha nodded, then turned to Cyrus again. "Let's play a song for them."

"Yeah!" Cyrus ran to the windows by the fireplace, where a standing piano faced the floor-to-ceiling panes. Natasha lifted the lid over the keys and pulled out the bench, placing Cyrus on her lap as she sat.

Leif curled into their chair, hugging the rice pack to their stomach. Tears pricked their eyes again, but not out of despair now. As Natasha and Cyrus coaxed a tune out of the piano, Leif felt the first semblance of comfort since this miserable day had started.

Maybe the misfortunes were done, then. Maybe this *would* be okay.

3



"WHO THE HELL ARE *YOU*?"

Leif jumped, nearly dropping the jars of herbs they had carefully balanced in their hands. They spun around and found a young woman in the doorway of the infirmary office. Leif knew without asking that this was Dr. Adriyen Snow.

She was younger than Leif had pictured—no more than a handful of years Leif's senior—and she was on the shorter side, with a stocky build and ample curves. Her ginger curls were bundled in a heap on top of her head, further corralled by a white bandana. She wore a dark blue skirt paired with a white blouse, and carried a basket stuffed with little bags and pouches. A silk cravat matching her skirt was tied snugly around her neck.

Leif carefully set their herbs down on the table and offered a hand. The doctor did not move. "M-My name is Leif Trysz? I'm an apothecary. Er...the Beldons' apothecary, now. I guess we'll be sharing an office?"

Dr. Snow's frown had deepened with every

word out of Leif's mouth, and now her eye twitched. "Sharing...an office?"

"Y-Yes? That's what Master Beldon told me." They flickered a nervous smile, unsure why the doctor was so put off by their presence. Their heart fluttered around like a manic bird in their chest. "I won't take up too much space, I promise, and I won't get in your way. I just need a place to—"

"*No.*" Adriyen finally stepped fully into the room. She dropped the basket next to the door; its contents clattered. "I work alone, kid. I don't care how little space you *think* you'll take up—you *will* be in my way, and I don't need to be tripping over you while I try to do my work. There's no room for you here, and sorry, the position of medical professional is already taken." She scoffed. "As if that's anything close to what you are. Go store your hallucinogenic drugs somewhere else."

"They're not— What? They're just herbs—"

"What's not clear?" Adriyen snapped, and for a moment she sounded so much like Leif's mother that they froze. "What part of *get out* don't you understand?" She shook her head, rubbing her temples. "Gods, I can't believe Master Beldon even let you through the front door. Throwing a goddamned quack at me...unbelievable. Why are you still here?"

Her sharp words—*get out*—echoed in Leif's mind, pinning them to the floor despite their instinct to flee. They didn't understand; what had they done wrong? They'd hardly moved anything or disturbed her impeccably organized supplies while they searched for a cabinet with enough space for the jars of herbs. They'd done as Master Beldon had told them, and explored the infirmary and its office to get an idea of where everything was, but they hadn't touched more than the cabinet doors. Why was Dr. Snow so angry? Why hadn't Master Beldon told her that Leif would be working with her?

"Going all puppy-eyes on me isn't going to change my mind," Adriyen snarled. "Get the hell out of my office, space girl."

Leif took a deep breath to clear their reeling mind and drew themself up taller. "I'll go, but can I just explain—"

"No! I have work to do! I don't have time for your—"

"You're not being fair!" Leif snapped. "Where else am I supposed to work?"

"Why is that my problem?" Adriyen pointed at the door. "Work in the garden, or in the goddamn attic, for all I care. Just not here."

Leif swallowed hard, then piled their jars of herbs in their arms and stormed across the room. Adriyen shouldered them as they passed her and the jars flew out of their hands, shattering and scattering across the floor.

They blinked at the mess, then looked up at Adriyen in numb shock.

"Oops." She smirked and sauntered off, crushing a few fronds of rosemary beneath her heel. When she looked back again and Leif still hadn't moved, she said, "Are you gonna clean that up?"

Face burning, Leif grabbed handfuls of all the herbs they could salvage, ignoring the bite of glass shards in their palms. They left the broken bottles and the dregs they couldn't scoop up, then darted out of the room.

Back in their attic room, Leif let their tears fall as they carefully picked tiny pieces of glass out of their palms. A bowl of pink-tinted water sat on the floor between their knees to catch the shards and occasional drops of blood, and they had a cleansing salve ready for when it was time to bandage their hands. The cuts stung, but it was nothing they couldn't handle.

They couldn't stop replaying the morning in their mind, and *that* hurt worse than their hands.

*Misfortunes come in threes*, they reminded themself. Maybe they'd miscounted yesterday; fainting from their nauseating menstrual cramps wasn't unusual, so maybe that didn't count as a misfortune. So that would make breaking the bowl, being kicked out of their home, and that terrible introduction to Adriyen their trio of misfortunes for the month. But did that also mean the good things about yesterday—meeting Natasha, meeting Cyrus, and listening to the song the two of them had played—didn't count, since they had interrupted the misfortunes? Shouldn't each set of threes happen consecutively?

Leif plucked the last visible piece of glass from the meat of their palm and flung it into the bowl, watching the water ripple from the impact. Their reflection wavered, blending their face with the shadows behind them. Sometimes Leif feared that this divination stuff was...unreliable. Their mother had raised them to be mindful and spiritual, to look for signs in the world around them and never write something off as a coincidence. She had said that the universe speaks to everyone, but only some knew how to listen.

Leif had strong intuition—they knew that as a fact—but they struggled to balance that intuition with an understanding of the world's endless nuances. Nothing ever had a simple meaning or a simple reason—least of all people's actions—but everything meant *something*. But when they could barely read the underlying tone in someone's voice or correctly interpret facial expressions, how were they ever supposed to find understanding in tea leaves or dreams?

What if it was all just...bullshit? What if all they were worth was a bitter cup of tea that worked because you believed it would? Was their entire practice—their lifelong expertise—just an elaborate placebo effect?

*Throwing a goddamn quack at me...*

Leif was the furthest thing from a doctor, and they weren't trying to be one, but calling them a quack was a step too far. They might doubt their divining abilities, but their apothecary skills were legitimate. Long before anyone had opened up a human body to see what was inside, people had been using herbs and teas to treat common illnesses. Leif's work was built on millennia of study and tradition, and of that, they were both fiercely proud and solemnly respectful.

Still, Leif winced at the echo of Adriyen's words in their mind. Part of them wished to never cross paths with her again, but they also wanted to make a different impression. Maybe if they caught her at a better time, when their presence wouldn't come as a surprise, she'd at least be able to tolerate them. Leif didn't expect an apology, but they were willing to work alongside her if she could manage to set her assumptions aside.

A soft knock from the door at the bottom of the stairs drew Leif out of their thoughts. "One moment!" They smeared the salve on their hands and quickly wrapped bandages around their palms, then grabbed a shawl and threw it over their shoulders as they hurried to the door. They found Natasha on the other side, bundled in a long wool coat, a fluffy scarf, and a fur hat.

Leif blinked a few times, and then their face flooded with heat as they remembered Natasha's promise for today. "Oh! We were going— I'm so sorry, I completely forgot."

"Is this a bad time?" Her eyes wandered down to their hands and she frowned. "Are you all right?"

Damn, she was perceptive. Leif tucked their hands under their arms. "It's nothing, just a small cut. Accident. Dropped something. I'm fine. Um... let me get my coat, and...You're sure it's okay for me to go with you?"

Natasha didn't look convinced about their hands, but she let it go. "Of course it is! Do you think Marcus can stop me?" A smirk curled at the corner of her mouth, but a shadow of something heavier darkened her eyes—just for a second, but Leif saw it. "We can leave a note that you're out for a while, if that'll make you feel better. Truly, I'd rather have the company, and shopping with my children is...like herding cats."

Leif smiled. "I can imagine. Right, I'll just be a second." They hurried back upstairs, grabbed their coat, tied their boots, and then joined Natasha out in the hallway.

Her smile turned a little strained. "Leif, it's cold out there. It was snowing this morning. Don't you have something warmer?"

Leif looked down at their old, well-worn linen jacket and shrugged. "No...I didn't, um, have time to grab anything else from home."

"Then we should stop at Nel's—"

"No!" Leif said, too loudly. They shrank back. "Sorry. No. That's okay. We're going shopping, right? I can buy a coat. Been meaning to, anyway."

Natasha eyed them closely, but didn't push the issue. "Very well. But take this, at least." She unwrapped her scarf and draped it over Leif's shoulders; they pulled it tighter to savor its warmth and caught a faint scent of something like cinnamon. "Better," Natasha declared. "Now come on, let's get out of this dreary old cave and see what the city has to offer us today."

4

LEIF LEANED against the window of the juddering carriage and watched the snow descend upon the High District. Fluffy flakes filled the air, swirling and dancing as they floated down to blanket the trees and houses. Aside from the rattle of wheels and the muffled clop of hooves, the streets were quiet, and for a few minutes, if they closed their eyes, Leif could forget about everything weighing them down.

"How did it go this morning, meeting Adriyen?" Natasha asked. She sat on the bench opposite them, face turned to the pale sunlight that broke through the clouds.

Leif's fleeting peace evaporated. They shrank back in their seat and ducked their head. "Not good. I didn't realize that she wasn't aware I'd be working with her, and...I think I surprised her, and she didn't take it well."

The more Leif thought about it, the less they could blame her, honestly. If they'd come back to their space to find someone poking through cabinets and making themselves at home, they'd react harshly too.

"I should have warned you that she can be... particular," Natasha said. "I'm surprised Marcus didn't—Well. I shouldn't be surprised that Marcus didn't say anything to her. I swear, sometimes he forgets she exists unless he needs her to patch him up." She sniffed. "Don't take it personally if you ever feel that way. Marcus has a one-track mind. The man thinks about vampires more than the vampires think about themselves."

Leif shrugged. "He's focused on his work. I'm no stranger to that." They recalled many days across their childhood where they wouldn't see their mother at all, save for a few quick glimpses as she hurried between her workroom and the shop. They'd learned quickly that if they didn't wish to go to bed hungry, they had to figure out how to make their own dinners.

Natasha pursed her lips. "That's putting it lightly. Anyway, I'm sure Adriyen will come around. I can speak to her, if you'd like."

Leif was certain that would make everything worse. Besides, they could take care of themself. "No, I can handle it. I *should've* handled it differently today, but I panicked." They rubbed their hands up their arms. "I don't always remember that sometimes people are just... unkind."

"You expect the best of people," Natasha said gently. "That's not a fault. And Adriyen isn't unkind, she's just stubborn. The more you speak to her, the more you'll see that her abrupt tone isn't personal. She's focused, too, and *very* serious about her work."

Leif winced and turned again to the window. They could believe that about Adriyen's personality, but shoving them so they dropped and ruined a bunch of their supplies was more than that. Leif was all too familiar with bullies, but they'd never had to endure living under the same roof as one.

Unless you counted their mother, which seemed both unfair and a bit dramatic.

"Did...something else happen?" Natasha asked in that careful tone that suggested she already knew the answer.

"No." Leif kept their eyes fixed on the snowy street outside. Before Natasha could press further, they changed the subject. "I'm sorry I snapped at you earlier, when you suggested we stop at my mother's house."

There was a notable pause; Leif could feel Natasha's eyes on them, but she said nothing.

"I can't go back." The words nearly got stuck on the way out, as if speaking them would make it truer than it already was. Leif swallowed hard and went on: "She didn't just...encourage me to come work for the Beldons. This wasn't me leaving the nest. She kicked me out."

Natasha's soft gasp made something tighten in Leif's chest. They caught themself flinching when she reached over and gently touched their knee.

"I don't know what she told you or Master Beldon," they whispered, fighting back tears, "but I'm here because she doesn't want me. All I'm good at is making tea and simple remedies, and that wasn't enough for her. Especially since I wasn't any good at numbers and got distracted when I was supposed to be minding the shop. I don't know what I'm doing, I don't even know if I can actually be useful to your family, but I don't— I don't have anywhere else to go."

Leif knew they shouldn't be telling her any of this. What better way to lose this one singular chance to survive on their own than to admit to the woman partially in charge of their fate that they didn't even really want to be here? *You're being too trusting again*, they scolded themself, and the snide voice sounded an awful lot like their mother. Yet there was something about Natasha, something warm and comforting that Leif had never seen in another person before. She made them feel at ease, and suddenly they couldn't keep anything bottled up.

Maybe this was their intuition at work: an irrational, inexplicable feeling that this woman was *safe*, and Leif didn't have to hide from her.

"Leif," she said softly, and their tears finally fell when they looked up at her. Sorrow creased her face, carving a little furrow between her eyebrows. "I'm so sorry, love. I suspected that Nel wasn't telling us the whole story when her demand for you to work for us came so suddenly, but I would never have guessed the truth of it."

Leif stared at her, and it was all they could do to stop themself from breaking down. Natasha *believed* them. Despite what she knew of Leif's mother, despite admitting that she owed the woman her life, she didn't brush off Leif's words with a scoff. Didn't assert that the endlessly selfless Nel Trysz would *never* exile her only child.

Leif was so used to people assuming that they had the life of a princess in their mother's home, wanting for nothing, showered with affection, that to speak the truth of it and not be laughed at was unfathomable.

And yet, there was nothing if not absolute sincerity in Natasha's green eyes. She cared about Leif. Somehow, after hardly a day, she cared about them more than their actual mother ever had.

"You're safe here." Natasha gently took Leif's hands and gave them a light squeeze. "I promise you that. Don't worry about Marcus, or even Adriyen. You will be taken care of, and it may not feel like it now, but this can be your home. It's just a matter of finding the people who make it feel like so."

Leif smiled, too choked up to speak. Natasha gently swiped her thumb across their cheek, clearing away their tears. Leif felt an overwhelming swell of affection for her, yet simultaneously a stab of envy that her children were lucky enough to have her as a mother. How different would their life be, how much less stormy would their mind be, if someone like Natasha had raised them? Nel had always told them to be more grateful for their fortunes, to consider that so many people had it worse than they did, and that they had no right to complain about anything when their mother kept a roof over their head and food in their belly. But was that not the bare minimum? Didn't every child also deserve love and care, not just basic necessities to keep them alive?

Leif would have given it all up—their talents, their apothecary skills, their study of the mystic—in exchange for a mother like Natasha. And if that made them ungrateful, well...they didn't see what was so wrong about being ungrateful for things that made their life harder.

The carriage slowed to a halt, and Natasha gave Leif's hands one last comforting squeeze before opening the door. Leif followed her, fixing the scarf around their neck as they stepped onto the snowy street.

# 5

LEIF HAD NEVER HAD much of an opportunity to explore Chestervale outside of the blocks surrounding their home, and while they and Natasha were still in the High District, they had come to a part of it that Leif had never seen. The trees that lined the curving road were decorated with shiny glass orbs, some of which housed tiny flickering candles that made the trees glow beneath their snowy coats. Gold ribbons and pine boughs adorned the streetlamps, and nearly every house they passed had an evergreen wreath on the door and candles in the windows. Leif assumed that much of it had been put up for Darkest Night, which had passed a couple of weeks ago, but most people left the evergreen adornments on their homes for all of winter—a welcome glimpse of verdant life as a reminder that the snow would melt and the earth would thaw.

Personally, Leif preferred winter over the other seasons. It was a quiet season, a time for reflection, when the world forced everyone to slow down. Leif loved the tranquility of it, the hush of snow settling on the trees. Scarcely were they happier than with a cup of tea and a book beside the fireplace while snow flurried outside.

Leif typically perceived Chestervale as being gray and gloomy in the colder months—which also compelled them to stay inside—but with a fresh blanket of snow cloaking the city, the busy streets seemed almost magical. Leif found themself smiling as they walked at Natasha's side, weaving around other pedestrians hurrying on their ways. They passed shops aglow with warm lights, bakeries with lines out the door, and bustling restaurants juggling the lunch rush. More than a few people smiled or tipped their hats to Natasha, and some greeted her by name. Curious eyes bounced to Leif before flicking away, the question hanging in the air but unvoiced by the well-dressed elite who were too well-trained to be outwardly nosy. Leif kept their head down, eyes fixed on the snowy sidewalk, and tried not to wonder what those people would speculate about them behind closed doors.

"Here we are." Natasha paused beneath a green-and-white-striped awning and pulled the door open for Leif, who quickly scurried inside. Warmth enveloped them, along with a mouthwatering, sugary aroma.

"Ahh, Mrs. Syll-Beldon!" A plump man with a fluffy beard waved from behind the counter. His tie was the same bright pink as the frosting on the cupcakes displayed to his left. "Good afternoon to you, madam!"

"Good afternoon, Mr. Wills." Natasha

approached the man and shook his hand with a smile. "How's business today?"

"Sold more hot cocoa than cookies, but can't complain!" He laughed, and his eyes gleamed as he gazed at Natasha. "It's good to see you. How are you doing?"

"Oh, same as always," Natasha said with a shrug. "The kids keep me busy, but they're back to their studies today, so I finally have some free time." She glanced over her shoulder at Leif, who hovered behind, pretending to inspect a display of brightly frosted cookies. "Leif, this is my friend, Mr. Wills. His pastry shop is the best in town. Mr. Wills, this is Leif. They're our family's new apothecary."

"That so!" Mr. Wills grinned. "Very good to meet you. Tell you what, any friend of Natasha's is a friend of mine. Pick something out for yourself, and it's on the house!"

Leif's eyes widened. "Oh, I...Are you sure, sir? I can—"

"I insist." He gestured toward his shop. "Anything you'd like."

Leif didn't know where to start. Their mother wasn't much of a baker, and when she went out to the shops it was always for practical things for the business or for her hearty meals. Not even for their birthdays did she bring them a cake or any kind of sugary treat. Sweets were nearly unheard of in her house, so rare that Leif didn't even know what some of these delights were.

While Natasha picked up a pie she had ordered, Leif finally settled on one of the pink-frosted cupcakes. They lost count of how many times they thanked Mr. Wills as they followed Natasha outside, and when they tried the cupcake they stopped fully in their tracks. The frosting was rich and creamy, the cake itself so light that it practically melted in their mouth. It was the most delicious thing Leif had ever tasted. They had half a mind to turn around and run back into the shop for another one. Or ten. Or one of everything that baker had to offer.

Natasha pulled Leif off to the side of the sidewalk so they weren't in the way. "Pretty good, isn't it? You've got to try this pie when we get home, too. The kids complained the first time I brought one of these home instead of making my own, but one bite had them all begging for Mr. Wills's pies for dessert every night." She chuckled, and the two of them set off down the sidewalk again.

"I just need to stop at the library, and then we can go see Mr. Simm at the furniture shop," Natasha said. "There's a chance we may have to order what you need, which means it'll be a week or so before the shop can deliver it, but we'll figure something out in the meantime if you'd rather not sleep in my parlor. I can probably convince Arthur to help me move a couch up to your attic."

Leif finished the cupcake and licked frosting off their thumb. "I really appreciate you doing this for me. It feels wrong, that you're going out of your way to help, but...I'm very grateful."

"It's no trouble at all, love," Natasha assured them. "You came to us with hardly more than the clothes on your back—which reminds me, we *will* be finding you a proper coat today—and it would be shameful of us to throw you into an empty room when you'll be providing a service to us. There's no excuse for you to be treated poorly when this family has more wealth and resources than half the population of Chestervale."

Leif didn't think they imagined the bitterness in her voice, and they couldn't disagree. They'd known the Beldons were wealthy, of course, but seeing that house had put it in a very different perspective. "Still...thank you."

Natasha glanced down at them with a warm smile, and affectionately squeezed their shoulder.

They continued along the curving road, passing more shops, restaurants, cafes, and a few pubs. Eventually the buildings gave way to a small park, its benches and lamp posts topped with fresh snow. People strolled hand-in-hand, some with dogs or small children, others wandering off the meandering trail to toss seeds to birds that braved the cold. Natasha turned into the park, greeting acquaintances along the way as she and Leif cut a path across the snow.

On the other side of a small, frozen pond, a grand columned building dominated the street opposite the park. Towering pines framed it on either side, and dozens of people milled up and down the steps leading to its entrance. Natasha led the way across the busy road and ascended the stairs, but Leif stumbled to a pause at the bottom.

"H-Hold on." Their mouth fell open as they gazed up at the words carved into the stone overhead: CHESTERVALE PUBLIC LIBRARY.

"Yes?" Natasha grinned.

"*This* is the library?"

"Welcome to the High District branch." Natasha nodded toward the doors. "Wait till you see the inside."

Leif hurried to follow her up the steps, and their jaw dropped all over again when they stepped inside the grand building. The main floor alone could have fit House Beldon snugly inside it, and three more stories cascaded upward to a central rotunda decorated with an elaborate mural. Leif could see only mere glimpses of the library's collection on the upper floors, but even still it was more books than they'd ever seen in their life. This was incredible. A person could get utterly lost in here.

They had to consciously tear their gaze back down to make sure they wouldn't walk into anyone or lose Natasha; they hurried to catch up with her as she approached a long, curving desk with five staffed stations. A young, fair-skinned person with dark hair that curled around their ears waved to Natasha and Leif with a smile. Leif felt a stab of envy at how effortlessly *neutral* they appeared; they were dressed fairly masculine, complete with a black vest and a purple cravat tied loosely around their neck, but something about them said "not a man" just as much as their style suggested "not a woman." When Leif and Natasha went up to the desk, Leif noted with satisfaction that the clerk's name tag had *they/them/theirs* written beneath their name.

"Hello there!" the clerk said. "What can I do for you?"

"I have a couple of books to pick up." Natasha passed them a white card bearing her signature beneath a stamp of the library's emblem. "Natasha Syll-Beldon."

The clerk nodded, then did a double-take and looked up at Natasha with new interest. "Sorry, did you say *Beldon*?"

Natasha's expression grew a bit strained. "I did, but please, think nothing of it."

"R-Right, of course, forgive me." The clerk darted through a doorway into a back room, and then returned a moment later with two books wrapped together beneath a folded paper bearing Natasha's name. "Here we are."

Leif's attention wandered to the rows of bookcases across the room, which displayed what they assumed to be newer additions to the collection. They itched to go over there and explore, but they hesitated; they didn't want to hinder Natasha's errands, especially when their next stop was for Leif specifically. So they watched the other patrons browse the books, making a mental note to come back here as soon as they could.

The library they'd frequented near their mother's house was far less grand than this. It was still technically in the High District, but closer to the city walls, where the streets were narrower and the buildings older and smaller than these freshened boutiques. Leif's usual library was tucked on one such street, a little cobbled structure with hardly as many books as this branch's new-release section. It was small and it was old, but the librarians there were kind, and their love for the place was clear. Leif had loved it, too, and suddenly longed to go back. They couldn't imagine this place being their go-to homely haven.

"Ready?" Natasha asked, tucking her books into the canvas bag she carried on her shoulder. "We can go to the furniture shop now, and then how about lunch?"

Leif's first instinct was to decline, to insist that they could manage their own lunch once they returned to the house, but as they headed out of the library and down the steps, they realized that Natasha had said it as a suggestion rather than an offer. So they resisted the reflex to deflect the kindness, and meant it when they said, "That sounds great."

Three hours later, Leif returned to House Beldon with a full belly, a new coat, and four pieces of bedroom furniture on order. Natasha had let them choose what they wanted—though Leif constrained themself to the plainest, least expensive models available—and when Natasha had signed the orders for a bedframe, a side table, an armchair, and a chest of drawers, the shop owner had assured her that the bed, at least, could be delivered later today.

Natasha, of course, hadn't stopped at mere furniture. She had taken Leif to three more shops, securing blankets, curtains, and an elegant oil lamp. When they'd returned to the mansion, she had woven through numerous rooms on the first and second floors, collecting other various household things that she insisted Leif would need, including an entire rug that she dragged out of a parlor. Leif could do nothing but watch and accept; every time they assured her that they had more than enough, she regarded the room thoughtfully for a minute before rushing off to grab something else.

Leif didn't know what to do with such kindness. They couldn't possibly repay this debt, but somehow they knew they wouldn't have to. Natasha wouldn't have gone to such lengths if she didn't truly want to, and...well, she had a point about the Beldons and their wealth. Besides, it wasn't as if Leif was taking any of this out of the house. If they left, the family would still have all of the furnishings.

When they'd set up their living space as best they could without the remaining furniture, all that was left to do was wait. And as much as they dreaded to do it, they went down to the infirmary and knocked on Adriyen's office door.

She was smiling when she opened it, but the expression fell immediately when she saw Leif. "Oh. You're still here."

"I want to apologize," Leif said.

"Okay, so do it."

"I'm— Can you just listen?"

"Listening. You're sorry for...spilling broken glass all over my office?" Adriyen raised a sharp eyebrow.

Leif took a deep breath. "No. Well, yes. I am sorry for that." *Even though that wasn't my fault.* "But I'm also sorry for intruding into your space. I shouldn't have come in here and tried to make room for myself without your knowledge."

"No, you shouldn't have. Is that all?"

"Um..." Leif searched for the right words. "Yes? But—"

"Great. I'm busy. Bye."

The door slammed in their face.

Leif growled a frustrated noise. "Seriously? Why are you like this?"

They didn't expect an answer, and they certainly didn't expect the door to burst open again. "Like *what*?" Adriyen snapped. "Assertive in my place here? Protective of my job and my space? I worked hard to get where I am, space girl. I've been learning medicine since I could read, and I passed every class, exam, and placement in the top percentage of my peers. I graduated with my degree two years earlier than usual, and the Beldons hired me without question. I *belong* here. I'm *needed* here. These people keep this city safe from monsters that would otherwise bleed us all dry, and without me, they can't do their jobs. So the last thing I need around me is a *quack* who gets high and looks at the stars and thinks they're speaking to her."

Leif burst out laughing. They couldn't help it. "That's what you think I do? You think this is all... hallucinations and psychedelics? You have *no idea* what you're talking about."

"What I *know* is that whatever you claim to do

as *medicine*"—she put the word in air quotes—"is an insult to my expertise, and to the science itself. I don't care what Master Beldon wants with you. You will *not* interfere with my work, there is *not* room for you in my office, and we will most certainly not be working together."

"Fine." Leif crossed their arms. "Forgive me for trying to be *friendly*. I didn't realize my very existence offended you."

"Well, now you know." Adriyen flicked a hand and turned on her heel. "Oh, and word to the wise, space girl: no one in this house is your friend. So enjoy Mrs. Beldon's obsession with you while you've got it, because it won't be long before she moves on."

She shut the office door before Leif could say another word.

Leif left and tried to shove the conversation out of mind. It was done, and it hadn't gone how they'd wanted, and it hadn't been productive, but there was nothing they could do. Yet Adriyen's warning haunted them through the halls. *It won't be long before she moves on.* As if Leif was something to be enjoyed and humored for a time and then cast aside. Thrown out. Forgotten. Natasha wouldn't do that to them...would she? How could she, after every kindness she had offered them? How was her generosity anything less than genuine?

The worries followed Leif all the way to the fourth floor. As they came upon the final landing, passing the narrow window there, movement from the grounds below caught their eye. A figure strode swiftly across the estate, cutting a path through the snow. Their back was to the house, but even from a distance, Leif recognized the mane of brown curls. Natasha.

It struck them as odd. They couldn't put their finger on why, but an instinct needled them nonetheless. She was moving too hurriedly to be simply out for a stroll; they could almost sense her urgency from here. Any quicker and she'd be running—though whether it was *to* something or *from* something, Leif couldn't say. Nor did they have a clue as to where she'd be heading; there was nothing beyond the trees surrounding the estate except for an old, ruined stone tower.

When Natasha disappeared from sight, swallowed by the trees, Leif tore themself away from the window and continued toward their quarters. The day was waning, and hopefully their bed would be delivered soon. Night, and the promise of sleep, couldn't come fast enough.

Days stretched into weeks, and Leif settled into their new life with smoother ease than they ever would have expected on that first day. Their attic space felt more like home every day, made cozy with tapestries, rugs, and scented candles that grew in number each time they ventured into town with Natasha.

Their new bed was far more comfortable than the lumpy thing they'd slept on at their mother's house, and the blankets Natasha had given them carried a subtle sent of lavender that lulled Leif into calm sleep each night. They rested soundly and dreamed beautifully, and their mind was clearer than ever.

Their kitchen had gradually come together into a somewhat useable space; it still needed some work, but they were able to begin and end their days with their favorite teas, which they were delighted to find in steady supply at the little market that gathered in the square down the street.

They didn't try to bargain with Adriyen again.

They found the supplies they needed and set up their apothecary in their kitchen, stocking one cabinet with herbs and another with remedies ready to go for anyone who needed them. Master Beldon had checked in with them only once, on the day they had agreed to start work, and he'd nodded approvingly when he'd seen the setup Leif had constructed. Leif had not seen him since, and they didn't expect more than that.

They spent their days buried in the books they'd brought from home, refreshing the studies their mother had expected of them all their life. They noted recipes for new remedies, and experimented with alternate ingredients in case there was ever an herb or seed they couldn't find. They'd have to wait until spring to start growing anything, but they listed everything they wanted to plant, hoping that their request for a patch of garden would be met with approval.

Little by little, they started to believe that they could do this. They could be a real apothecary, not just a clumsy shop assistant.

All they needed now was for someone in the family to actually need something from them.

They'd finally met all of the Beldons by now: Cyrus, the youngest, was most frequently in Natasha's company, while the three older children —twins Poppy and Joel and the eldest, Arthur— spent the majority of their days flocked together. Leif didn't know much about them or what they did all day; it was clear that they didn't go to school, but rather had private tutors and presumably learned their trades as hunters alongside a general education.

Leif had been shocked—and startled—to meet Marcus's brother, Emerson, entirely by accident one evening as they'd passed by a nondescript door on the first floor only for it to fly open and present a Beldon they'd not yet seen. Emerson was an alchemist, and spent many long hours in his laboratory in the cellar when he wasn't schooling the children in vampire physiology.

Marcus himself was rarely home, and when he was, he secluded himself in his office in the east wing of the mansion. Leif occasionally glimpsed visitors—well-dressed folks of the same social caliber as the Beldons—but Leif was expected to stay clear of Master Beldon's work, and they did so gladly.

So, it seemed, did the rest of the family; Leif didn't want to make any assumptions, but it rather appeared that everyone went out of their way to avoid the master of the house.

It was all the same to Leif. Marcus Beldon's reputation preceded him; Leif had known who he was and what he did for as long as they could remember. The name Beldon—alongside Sheridan and Barlow—lurked in the back of every Chestervale citizen's mind; they were the peacekeepers, the experts on all things monstrous, the heroes who made it their duty to know their enemies and how to kill them. Leif didn't have any particularly strong worries about vampires, but perhaps they ought to thank the Beldons for that. In a city co-inhabited by five ancient vampire families, Leif supposed it was better to have the hunters than not have them.

"You're quiet tonight," Natasha remarked as she poured them a cup of tea. Unintentionally, the two of them had made it a sort of ritual to have tea in Natasha's parlor every night—a room, Leif noted, that she did not share with Marcus. But they pretended not to notice the evidence that she sometimes slept here and the fact that it was one of very few locked rooms in this house, and enjoyed the evenings for their comfort and conversation.

Tonight, however, Leif couldn't find much to say.

"What's on your mind?" Natasha asked.

Leif lifted a shoulder. Really, nothing in particular. They were content, and ironically, maybe that was what weighed on them. Despite this mansion gradually starting to feel like home, part of them was still waiting for the other shoe to drop.

Their eyes slid back into focus and they realized they'd been staring at the portrait that hung over the fireplace: a bright image of two smiling women with a little girl between them. One had golden hair and a fair, rosy face, and the other had a warm brown complexion and a head of curls that matched the child's, as well as green eyes that Leif would know anywhere.

Natasha followed their gaze. "My mothers," she murmured. "That painting is one of the last pieces of my home that I have. I insisted that it came with me when I married Marcus; I couldn't bear to part with it, even if he thought me immature for holding onto my past." She stirred her tea, eyes distant. "Mum—the one on the left, with the blonde hair—fell ill very soon after this portrait was finished. We lost her within weeks. None of us had any idea this would be our last image of her."

Leif turned their head toward her. "I'm so sorry. You were so young..."

Natasha looked down at the teacup in her hands. "We made do. It wasn't easy. My surviving mother tried to hide it from me, but I knew she was struggling. We moved from the east coast and started over here in the city, where an aunt I'd never met had married into the Sheridan family. She made sure that my mother and I wanted for nothing, but..." She sighed. "It was a blessing and a curse. By the time I'd grown up, Mama had gotten comfortable in our high-class lifestyle, and suddenly it was up to me to ensure we kept it. Party after party, ball after ball, dinner after dinner...all to secure a wealthy spouse for me."

"Did you want that?" Leif asked. "To marry?"

"I did...in theory. In the way all romantics dream of marriage: a faraway fantasy. The most magical day of their lives." Natasha let her head fall against the cushioned back of the chair. "I evaded the suitors for as long as I could. Oh, the fights Mama and I had... But then Marcus Beldon noticed me, and it was all over. Suddenly my choice in the matter was gone, as if it'd never been there at all. My mother saw the newly confirmed head of the most influential—and *wealthiest*—hunter family express interest in me, and she could see no outcome other than my marriage to him."

She sniffed and glanced at Leif. "He's twelve years older than me. Did you know that? He doesn't look it—not yet, anyway—but to me, at nineteen, he might as well have been my father. But such a gap wasn't *technically* inappropriate since I was of age—*it could be worse*, people said—so when Marcus asked for my hand...I said yes. I didn't want to, but I knew I would make things worse for myself if I refused. I didn't want to turn my back on my mother. She was all I had left, and I hated the animosity that had been between us. I did want her to have a comfortable life, so I gave up mine. And here I am."

Natasha's gaze wandered back up to the portrait, but Leif could see that she was miles away. She lifted her cup as if toasting the painted figures. "Hope you're happy, Mama. Hope you're happy."

Leif swallowed a sip of tea, unsure what to say —if there was even an appropriate thing *to* say. In their experience, conversations like this happened when a person needed to let go of something they'd been keeping bottled up for a long time. Maybe Natasha simply needed someone to listen.

"Are...you happy?" Leif hazarded after several quiet minutes.

Silence yawned between them, and Leif would've accepted that as answer enough. "I...find happiness where I can. In the things that are precious to me. Cyrus, Poppy, Joel, Arthur—even though he's fifteen and therefore I'm his enemy." She smiled a little. "My music, my drawings, my garden...I remind myself every day that these things make my life beautiful, and they're worth living for."

Leif watched a bit of tea leaf float around in their cup. "Can I admit something?"

"Of course," Natasha said.

"I've rarely had things like that in my life," they said softly. "If you'd asked me a few months ago, I'd struggle to name even three things I loved enough to look forward to every day. I thought it would worsen when I came here, since I had nothing and no one." Leif looked up at Natasha and smiled. "But it didn't worsen, because of you. You gave me a reason to *want* to be here. You remind me every day that for every cruelty in this world, there are a thousand kindnesses to outnumber it."

Natasha stared at them, lips tight and eyes intense. She opened her mouth, only to close it again. Her brows twitched as if struggling against a frown.

Leif ducked their head, pushing their hair behind their ears. "S-Sorry, that's—"

They froze when they suddenly found Natasha's arms around them.

Tears welled in Leif's eyes and quickly spilled over. They gingerly slid their arms around Natasha, letting their head fall against her chest. Her arms were warm and strong around them, and the faint, familiar scent of cinnamon and cranberries surrounded them.

When was the last time their mother had hugged them? Had she, ever, since Leif had grown up? Once they'd let go of their childhood clinginess, had she hugged them, even once?

Leif truly did not know. If she had, it was not within their conscious memory. A strange sense of loss overcame them then, and they hugged Natasha tighter, burying their face into her soft sweater. *Savor this*, said that lonesome voice within them. *Savor this so that you don't forget.*

When Natasha finally let go after several long, tranquil moments, her eyes glistened with tears. "Thank you," she rasped. "I hope I didn't startle you or cross a line by hugging you. What you said means a lot to me, more than I can express in words. And I feel very much the same about you, Leif. I hope it's not too much to say that I care for you every bit the same as one of my children."

Leif couldn't say why those words struck them harder than even the unexpected hug, but a sob burst out of them without warning. Heavy, silent shudders wracked their body until they couldn't hold them in any longer. Yet even as they gasped for air, it wasn't panic or sorrow that gripped them; rather, they felt a weight leave them as they cried. Natasha gathered them into her arms again, wrapping them in a warm embrace until Leif calmed.

As the storm passed, they felt the absence of that weight they'd been carrying all their life, now replaced by a new, cathartic warmth:

They weren't unlovable.

Their mother didn't love them, but that did not mean no one could. Suddenly it was easier to accept the lack of love from Nel Trysz now that they knew it could come from someone else. Someone who saw them as a person to be cared for, not merely a business asset with clumsy hands.

Leif would stay in House Beldon forever if it meant they would be loved.

Later, Leif returned to their rooms and shouldered through the lower door, only to trip over a stack of boxes that crowded the entry room. Frowning, they pushed the boxes closer to the wall and shuffled around them to get to the stairs. What was all of this? It hadn't been here earlier. The boxes were unlabeled and apparently unopened, but Leif wasn't expecting any more deliveries, and Natasha would have told them if she'd ordered anything else. Or, at the very least, she wouldn't just leave stuff scattered in the middle of the entryway.

Leif made a mental note to ask about it tomorrow, and continued up into their flat.

They woke up early the next morning to muffled banging coming from the stairwell. They knew by the faint light filtering through the covered windows that it was far earlier than they needed to be awake; they pulled a blanket over their head and rolled over, resigned to ignore the noise. But when it persisted, preventing them from falling back to sleep, they finally flung off the covers and climbed down from the loft. They wrenched open their door and peered down the spiral stairs; below, they could see someone moving the boxes around—and bringing in more.

"Hello?" Leif called.

They shouldn't have been surprised when it was Adriyen who stepped into view. "Oh. Hello."

Leif went down the first few steps, wincing at the bite of cold metal on their bare feet. "What are you doing? What is all of this?"

"Things I don't have room for in my office." Adriyen shrugged. "Extra supplies, mostly. Sheets for the beds in the recovery room. Blankets. Robes, aprons. Why do you care?"

"Why are you putting it *here*?" Leif snapped.

Adriyen spread her hands and gestured to the space around her. "This is the attic. It's for storage."

"It's my house!"

"False. It's Master Beldon's house." Adriyen arched an eyebrow. "And just because he shoved you up in the attic doesn't make this any less of an attic. Look, it's not like I'm intruding into your actual living space. It's all staying down here."

"And I'm supposed to thank you for that?" Leif gripped the railing until their hands ached. "You had room for all of this in your office before. Take it back."

Adriyen planted her hands on her hips. "I reorganized. None of this needs to be in my office. Can you just let me do my job? It's not even in your way!"

"It *is* in my way!" Leif couldn't keep an angry

tremble out of their voice. They took a deep breath. "If it's not gone by the end of the day—"

"What?" Adriyen goaded. "What're you gonna do? Cry to Mrs. Beldon? What's *she* going to do?" Adriyen chuckled dryly and spun on her heel, striding toward the lower door. "Deal with it, space girl."

She slammed the door behind her before Leif could respond.

They inhaled another deep breath, then let it out in a growl. Hot tears prickled in the corners of their eyes, but they rubbed them away. That selfish physician would *not* make them cry again. *Pull it together, Leif.* They weren't a child. They couldn't expect to be rescued every time someone was rude to them. No, they needed to put their own foot down. Adriyen would never respect them if they didn't.

Leif didn't need—or want—Adriyen to like them. Gods knew they couldn't fathom ever liking her. But they did want her respect, if not as a practitioner of medicine, then at least as a professional, regardless of how little she understood their expertise.

Leif darted back upstairs only long enough to put proper clothes on, then stomped back down to the lower room and considered the boxes. Twelve large wooden cubes sprawled across the narrow space, placed at random, as if Adriyen had dropped them without a thought to organization. Leif itched to pack them all neatly into a corner, but no. That would be like rolling over and letting Adriyen have her way. No, the boxes were *not* here to stay.

The attic might be Leif's actual living space, but this room was still part of it, and still *theirs*. They'd spent their entire life sequestered in a corner of a house that wasn't theirs, with barely an inch to call their own. They weren't about to let a petty, insecure doctor take this from them.

The boxes were big, but most of them had holes in the sides that served as handles. Leif tested one and found it to be a manageable weight. Some were heavier, but they could comfortably carry even the biggest one across the room. They hefted one into their arms and started toward the door, but then an idea struck them.

Piling the boxes in the hallway wouldn't accomplish anything other than giving the staff more work. It wouldn't prove anything, especially not to Adriyen. But if they waited until tonight...

There must be *some* place for all this stuff in her office, right?

7

Leif buzzed with anticipation and anxiety as they went down to the second floor to meet Natasha for evening tea. They didn't want her to catch on that Adriyen had gotten on their nerves again, and especially not that they were up to something—they knew she'd be disappointed in them for being petty, which only made Leif's guilt about the whole thing worse. It occurred to them as they reached the second floor that they could skip tea altogether, but then Natasha would *really* be suspicious, so they strolled down the hall to her parlor and tried to put Adriyen out of mind.

They knocked lightly before stepping into the room, but apparently they were still too quiet; Natasha visibly jumped, jerking her head toward the door as she stumbled to her feet. Leif halted, stunned by the wild terror in her eyes. It was unlike anything they'd ever seen on her face.

"Natasha?" they whispered.

"Leif." Their name came out in a soft breath. She cleared her throat, but even when she spoke normally, her voice was strained. "M-My apologies. Come in. You startled me, that's all. I'm afraid I'm...a bit out of sorts tonight."

Leif didn't move from the threshold. "Should I... Should I go? Is this a bad time?"

"No, no, please." Natasha pushed her hair behind her ears, and Leif failed to stifle a gasp.

What they'd thought, at first, was a shadow across the right side of her face, was in truth a gruesome bruise that purpled the hollow around her eye and the top of her cheekbone.

Natasha hurriedly turned away, hiding the injured side of her face behind her hair. She masked the motion by turning to ring for tea, but Leif saw the way her hands shook as she rang the little silver bell.

They felt sick. Suddenly their feud with Adriyen seemed stupid and childish, and her unfair unkindness toward them was nothing compared to — Well. No, they didn't know what—or who—had left Natasha with such a bruise, but her unease and her desperation to hide the injury were all Leif needed to draw their conclusion.

Still, they needed to be certain. "Who did that to you?"

Natasha's hands stilled their fretting over the objects on the coffee table. She cast a quick glance at Leif before turning her face away. "Don't worry yourself, love. I'm fine. N-No harm done."

But Leif had heard the way her voice had started to tremble. Their heart thumped an anxious beat. "Natasha, if—"

A soft knock cut them off, and a servant

appeared then with a silver tray bearing a teapot and two cups. Natasha nodded gratefully as the woman placed the set on the table. In moments she had departed, and silence fell upon the parlor like a stifling blanket.

"Natasha," Leif tried again, "if someone—"

"Leif, I said I'm *fine*."

They shut their mouth, heart in their throat. She'd never snapped at them like that before.

Tense, silent seconds crackled by, and then Natasha sighed. "Come sit." She gestured at Leif's usual chair, then sank into her own without waiting for them to accept the invitation. They hovered by the fireplace for another minute, then finally conceded. Though when they sat it might as well have been upon thorns.

Natasha poured her tea, and all Leif could see was how severely her hands trembled; all they could hear was the slight clatter of the teapot's lid as she held it in place. When she started to lift her cup, her hands shook badly enough that the tea spilled over the rim; she all but dropped the cup, placing it harshly on the saucer with an abrupt *clack*.

She sank her head into her hands and let out a single, muffled sob.

Leif didn't even dare to take a breath. They didn't know what to do. What *could* they do? This was far outside the range of their knowledge; it was Adriyen who handled injuries, but would she even hear them out if they asked for her help? Would Natasha even want them to? Would that make everything worse?

But how could Leif *not* help? They'd grown to

love Natasha as the mother they'd never had; they couldn't ignore her of all people when she was in pain.

*And you know damned well it's not the bruise that's causing her pain*, said a voice in their head that had far more confidence than they. *You're here to soothe their pain. So do it.*

Leif slowly stood up from their seat. "I'll be right back. I promise."

They took off at a sprint the moment they were out of the parlor. Their surroundings passed in a blur as they dashed up the stairs, and only when they reached their stock of teas did they gain awareness of what was in front of them. Even then, they saw only what they needed: that herb, this flower, a teaspoon of sugar.

Leif collected everything in a bowl, grabbed an empty teapot, and then ran back down the stairs. They slowed when they reached the parlor and entered with purpose, but not hurriedly. Their heart might be racing, but there was no need to let their anxiety bleed into the room.

They knelt on the floor next to the table and let the leaves and petals steep, then poured it into the empty teacup that was meant to be theirs. Giving it a stir, they added another pinch of sugar and a drop of milk, and with steady hands, they offered the cup to Natasha.

"Drink this," they said softly. "It'll help."

Natasha swallowed thickly and wrapped her hands around Leif's so they cradled the cup together. Leif helped her guide it to her lips, and gently let go when she tipped it to take a sip. When she lowered the cup she took a slow, steadying breath and let the tension out of her shoulders.

Leif hadn't realized how drawn up she'd been until she started to relax. Her face cleared, little by little, and the tremor in her hands eased. They placed their hand on her knee and remained on the floor until she'd finished the tea; when she set the cup back on the table, she leaned forward and gathered them into a hug.

Leif held her fiercely, as if something in them thought it would be the last time they'd ever feel her arms around them.

Leif stayed with Natasha late into the night. Though they didn't talk—Natasha softly asked if they might simply sit in each other's company, she busying herself with a knitting project and Leif paging through a book of poems—Leif felt better by the time they parted ways, and they could tell that she did too. Her smile was still faint as she said goodnight, but it was warmer than before. Tired, yet genuine. All things considered, it was an improvement.

They'd nearly forgotten about the boxes crowding their entry room until they walked into one, catching the smallest toe of their left foot on its corner. They swore under their breath and shoved the box away, but the damage was done; their calm mood evaporated, and suddenly their petty scheme from earlier absolutely did matter.

They dragged the boxes out into the hallway, then grabbed one and carried it down the stairs, all the way to the first floor. The halls of House Beldon were darkened but never truly slumbering; the occasional oil lamp kept watch over the shadowed corridors, spilling pools of golden light on the polished floors. Leif hurried toward the infirmary on silent steps and relished their luck that they hadn't encountered any servants that might be wandering about.

Their resolve wavered when they reached the infirmary office. The room was dark behind the frosted glass pane, everything set to rest for the night. Adriyen's personal quarters were somewhere on the third floor—Leif didn't know precisely where—but still, some irrational part of them feared she'd somehow sense a disturbance to her work space.

Leif asked themself one more time if this was really worth it, then tried the doorknob. It turned, granting them graciously silent entry into the darkened office. They placed the first box against the wall beside the doors leading into the examination room, not *quite* in the way, and one who didn't know better might assume it was in its proper spot.

Then they went back up to the fourth floor, and one by one, hour by hour, they brought every single box down and scattered them around Adriyen's office. They shoved other things to the side and stacked other items on top of the boxes to make room. Every single crate had a space, just as Leif had expected.

By the time they placed the last one, their back ached, their arms felt like jelly, sweat slicked their forehead, and it was after dawn. They dragged themself back up to their rooms one last time, shouldered through the lower door, trudged up the spiral stairs, and only made it to the couch before they collapsed. Sleep took them immediately.

Leif felt like they'd only closed their eyes for a minute when they jolted awake at the sound of loud banging. It took them a second to realize it was coming from downstairs, and another second to remember why they were on the couch instead of in their bed. The stiff ache in their muscles, however, reminded them at once of their escapade last night.

And now the consequences had come knocking.

"I know you're up there!" Adriyen's voice all but shook the walls, even muffled behind two doors. "Is this your idea of a joke? Get the *hell* down here, space girl. We need to talk!"

Leif stormed across the room and went out to the stairwell, but only descended the staircase halfway. "First of all, stop calling me that. I'm not a girl. If you're going to be rude to me, at least spare me the courtesy of not misgendering me."

"Rude to *you*?" Adriyen shouted from the other side of the lower door. Leif was vaguely surprised she hadn't barged in, before they remembered that they'd slid the bolt on their way back in last night. "You think I've been *rude* to you?" Adriyen's fist slammed into the door again, and Leif involuntarily jumped.

They went down the rest of the stairs and approached the door. "You think that intruding into my living space and leaving your extra stuff all over the place *isn't* rude?"

Finally, they opened the door, revealing a red-faced, disheveled doctor. The sight of her momentarily shocked Leif; her hair was in disarray, half-up and half-down, her clothes were rumpled, and her hands were visibly shaking. It was such a stark difference to her usual collected demeanor that Leif almost offered her a cup of calming tea.

And yet, they couldn't quite find it in them to feel guilty for being the cause of her distress.

"If *that* was rude, then how would you describe what you pulled on me last night!" Adriyen flung a hand toward the hallway behind her, gesturing in the vague direction of the infirmary. "My office is a *disaster*. I spent *hours* tearing the whole room apart and putting everything back where it belongs, and even still there's more to put away. What the *fuck* is wrong with you!"

"I'm not sure what you mean." Leif crossed their arms. "Everything *was* put away. See, I told you there was room for the boxes. Now you've just created more work for yourself."

Adriyen stamped her foot, and if Leif wasn't genuinely nervous about her temper, it might've been kind of adorable—that is, in the way toddlers were when they didn't get their way. "Everything in that office was meticulously placed so I knew *exactly* where to find what I need. It was neat, organized, and uncluttered. I don't have *time* to figure out where you carelessly shoved everything, and I certainly don't have time to reset everything precisely how it was."

When Leif didn't respond, she curled her lip. "I keep this family *alive*. What part of that hasn't gotten through your thick skull? My ability to easily find my tools could be the difference between life and death for these people—for these *children*. Do you really want to be the reason I lose one of them? Do you want that on your conscience, just for the sake of a stupid prank?"

Leif almost backed down then, but though her voice had lost some of its ire, when Leif looked into her eyes, that venomous animosity reigned over the mask of concern that laced her voice. She was bluffing. Exaggerating. Sure, the Beldons had a dangerous job, and sure, there was no doubt of a physician's importance, but that was just it: Adriyen was a *physician*, not a surgeon. It was unlikely she would ever have a bleeding, dying child on her examination table.

"You're so full of shit," Leif scoffed, and turned their back on her. "Have fun reorganizing. And if you'd be so kind, Doctor, stay the hell out of my rooms."

They flung the door shut, cutting off the protest she'd started to make, and slid the bolt home.

# 8

THE NEXT DAYS brought outright war, but Leif had expected that. They were almost unsurprised to return to a damp, frigid room one afternoon after they'd—foolishly—forgotten to lock the attic door and found that Adriyen had left all the windows open. After burning through most of their own firewood to get the space back to its usual temperature, they calmly went down to Adriyen's office and stole her entire supply of wood.

They got in the habit of double-checking the lock on the attic door every time they left, and at night they pushed a chair in front of the door leading into their flat so that even if Adriyen got past the lower entry, she couldn't get into their home. When one morning they found themself trapped, the door barricaded from the outside, it had taken them three hours to nudge the obstructing crates and chairs enough to squeeze themself out.

They locked Adriyen out of her office the next

day. Their only regret was that they hadn't seen her reaction—or how she'd managed to get back in.

On and on it went—a bitter leaf in her coffee (which Leif had found foolishly unattended), a rotten onion hidden by their door (it took days for the odor to fade), fake messages to waste her time, stolen shoes—for over a week. And then Adriyen pushed it too far.

Leif encountered her on the stairs as she was going up to the third floor and they were heading down to the first. Their arms were full of books, the stack balanced precariously against their chest in such a way that they could just barely see where they were placing their feet. They fully intended to ignore Adriyen and continue their way toward the library.

They didn't see her move, but next thing they knew, they were tumbling. Books rained around them, and when the railing on the second-floor landing caught them, they'd left a trail of fallen volumes in their wake.

Leif dragged themself upright, wincing as their wrists smarted when they put weight on their hands. Their shoulder throbbed where it had collided with the banister, but they seemed to have spared their head.

Gritting their teeth, they glared up at Adriyen, who stood on the third floor landing with her shoulders thrown back as if she was the master of the house. "Watch where you're going next time." She tucked a stray curl behind her ear, then sauntered away.

Leif took a deep breath, and then another,

struggling to swallow back the anger that erupted within them. The telltale prickle of tears burned in their eyes and they squeezed them shut, taking another heavy breath.

They hated this. They hated *her*. Why couldn't she just ignore them? Why did their entire goddamned life have to be a battle just to survive? Why did there *always* have to be something horrid lurking behind every good thing? Why didn't they deserve to be safe? Why didn't they deserve to be *happy*?

"Leif? Goodness, are you okay?"

Rapid footsteps ascended the stairs, and Leif knew without looking up that the gentle hand that settled on their arm was Natasha's. "What happened?"

Leif took a shaky breath and opened their eyes, but did not look at Natasha. "I fell. I'm fine. Tried to carry too many books."

They could feel her eyes on them, waiting for them to go on, as if she knew there was more to it than a simple fall. Leif risked a glance at her and almost resolved to tell her the truth when the truth in question appeared once again at the top of the stairs.

Leif didn't know what Natasha saw in their eyes, but she looked from them to Adriyen and back to them, and a stony frown darkened her face.

Natasha rose to her feet. "Dr. Snow."

"Mrs. Syll-Beldon." Adriyen bowed her head.

"Do you have a minute, Doctor? Would you mind helping me collect these books?" She grabbed the few that had tumbled down to the landing and stacked them in her arms.

Leif became conscious of how much they were shaking. They didn't take their eyes off Natasha, loath to look at Adriyen and the contempt they knew they'd see on her face. The seconds that stretched between Natasha's request and Adriyen's reply were agonizing, and Leif wished they could sink into the floor.

This was going to make everything much, much worse if Leif didn't put a stop to it.

"Of course, ma'am." Adriyen smiled, but the painted lips of a doll would have been more sincere than the cold curl of her mouth. She gathered the books as she came down to the landing where Leif sat. They couldn't stop themself from flinching when she dropped the stack beside them.

"Thank you, Doctor," Natasha said. "That'll be all."

Adriyen nodded and turned away, but Leif did not miss the glare she flicked at them before heading downstairs.

Natasha waited until her footsteps had faded from earshot, and then helped Leif to their feet. "Are you hurt?"

They kept their eyes on the floor and bit their tongue against the first snappish response that came to mind: *And if I was, would you expect me to go to* her?

"No," they muttered.

"Did she push you?"

Leif swallowed. "No."

"Leif." Natasha's voice dipped chillingly low,

deathly serious. Leif had only ever heard her speak this way to her children, and for once being treated like one of them did not make Leif feel better. Only smaller. "I know you're strong, I know you're not a child, and I know you can take care of yourself. But if you feel unsafe in this house—"

"Unsafe?" Leif jerked back from her. "You're concerned about *me* being unsafe, when you—" Their eyes flicked to the fading bruise on her cheek. "Don't worry about me. Please. Adriyen is just a bully; I've dealt with worse. And if you say something to her or to Master Beldon, she's going to *get* worse. So please, just...just leave it alone."

"Leif—"

They ignored her, grabbed the books, and dashed down the stairs.

Leif knew they wouldn't be able to hide from Natasha for long; sure enough, she found them about an hour later in the conservatory, where they'd gone with the intention to sketch the plants and turn off their brain. But they had gotten no farther than opening their sketchbook; their thoughts refused to settle.

"This is one of my favorite rooms in this miserable old place." Natasha approached Leif casually, as if her presence was a coincidence. Her eyes drifted around the room, gazing at the flowering trees. "I like drawing the plants. I've always found botanical illustrations fascinating. I used to spend full days in here with my easel and canvas, dozens of paints spread out around me."

Her smile turned wistful. "Even if I had time to paint now, I haven't the energy. Sometimes even a few sketches seem like too much work."

Leif fiddled with their pencil. They knew that struggle well.

Natasha finally looked at them directly. "Marcus wants to speak with you."

Leif's blood ran cold. "What? Why?"

"He didn't say." Natasha's eyes darted to the floor. "I thought it best if I told you, rather than him."

Leif had half a mind to refuse the summons, but they knew that would make things *catastrophically* worse. It took them a minute to gather the courage to stand, and they trembled with nerves as they followed Natasha out of the conservatory and across the main floor...to Adriyen's office.

Oh, no.

So this *was* about the incident earlier. How could Natasha have betrayed them like that? And to *Marcus*? And now he— What, would scold Adriyen in front of Leif? That wasn't fair. That was wrong.

But what choice did they have? They braced themself and followed Natasha into the infirmary.

Adriyen was across the room, leaning on one of the doors leading into the examination room. Marcus stood in front of the windows with his hands behind his back. He turned his head when

Natasha and Leif entered, his cold eyes utterly inscrutable.

"Right. Let's settle this." Marcus's gruff voice sounded almost...*bored*. "I understand there is some animosity between the two of you." His eyes slid back to Adriyen.

"Yes, sir," she said, and Leif echoed the words in a mumble. Adriyen plowed on: "If I may, there's hardly need for an apothecary alongside my work. And on a practical level, there's no room for one, either. I made that quite clear to Leif, yet they have seemingly done everything in their power to get in my way and interfere with my ability to do my job."

Leif's mouth fell open, but they bit their tongue.

"Indeed, this isn't the first time you've expressed such a complaint about our apothecary." Marcus turned his head toward Leif. "Are you not satisfied?"

"I—"

"Did I not welcome you into our home when you would otherwise have been on the streets?" Marcus's blue eyes pinned Leif in place like a butterfly on a board. "Do you not have all of your needs met, beyond even what I would have deemed acceptable?"

"Y-Yes—"

Marcus turned fully to them. He wasn't an exceptionally tall man, but in that moment he seemed to fill the entire room. "Then I expect you, a servant of House Beldon, to do your work and serve this family without hindering the work of others.

Certainly not mine, and certainly not our doctor's." He leaned closer to them, and Leif's vision tunneled until his stony, weathered visage was all they could see. "Consider this your one warning, Leif Trysz. Your mother owes me no other favors, so I have no qualms about terminating your employment—"

"Marcus!" Natasha exclaimed.

"*Should the need arise,*" Marcus finished in a hiss, slicing a glare toward Natasha.

She wasn't deterred. "Marcus, do you really—"

"Enough," he snapped, and she flinched. Apparently satisfied, Marcus backed a step away from Leif and swiveled to look at Adriyen. "Are we understood? No more nonsense. You're adults; act like it. I do not wish to hear of further issues between the two of you."

Adriyen bowed her head. "Yes, sir."

"Yes, sir," Leif rasped.

"Splendid." Marcus nodded decisively, and then strode toward the door. "Good day, Doctor. Leif. Come, Natasha."

She followed him without hesitation, and it was only after the office door had clicked shut that Leif released the breath they'd been holding. All of the tension bled out of them, and they collapsed into a chair by the windows with their head in their hands. They didn't care that Adriyen was right there. They didn't even care to leave. Marcus's harsh voice thrummed in their mind like a drumbeat, bellowing a thunderous warning that they should never have gotten too comfortable here.

"Hey, um..." Adriyen's voice broke through

Leif's spiraling mind. "I didn't think he'd react like that. It was wrong of him to pin the blame solely on you."

Leif jerked their head up. "And what has suddenly made you realize that if not for *your* pettiness, we could have blissfully ignored each other this whole time? Was it hearing that I have nowhere else to go that changed your mind? Or maybe that my own mother kicked me out of her house and threw me here without a second thought? I don't need your fucking pity, Doctor." They stood to leave.

"Wait." Adriyen took a step closer to them. "First of all, I wasn't the only one being petty. Secondly, I'm not trying to pity you. But...I didn't know your situation. I thought..." She sighed and turned her head, fiddling with the stone pendant around her neck. "Well, it doesn't matter what I thought. I judged you cruelly and needlessly, and I am sorry. I never would have gotten Marcus involved if I'd known he'd threaten to take your job."

Leif wasn't buying it. If she genuinely felt bad, she was doing a poor job of showing it. "You told him there isn't space for me here. That sounds rather a lot like you wanted him to get rid of me." Leif scoffed. "And you made that wish very clear from the beginning."

Adriyen shrugged helplessly. "I...I'm sorry. I don't have an excuse. I don't even expect your forgiveness. I just—"

"Good," Leif cut her off, backing toward the door. "Because you're not going to get it. But I'm done with the stupid games, so you can rest assured that I will no longer be in your way as long as you stay out of mine."

"Leif, wait."

They wrenched the door open, only to immediately collide with Arthur Beldon—who all but collapsed into Leif. They jerked back, startled, and that was when they saw all the blood.

# 9

"ARTHUR?" Adriyen rushed to him and wrapped an arm around his waist to hold him up, but then his legs buckled and she only barely managed to catch him. "Gods have mercy," she muttered. "Leif, grab his legs—*gently*—and help me carry him into the examination room. First table. Ready?"

Leif hurried to help and held Arthur's legs as carefully as they could as they followed Adriyen into the next room. Arthur's breaths were erratic, each one edged with a pained whimper. He groaned through his teeth as Leif and Adriyen settled him on the table; Leif gave his hand a comforting squeeze as Adriyen rushed to put on a clean apron.

"Leif, grab a towel from that basket next to the sink and keep pressure on anything that's still bleeding. Arthur, take a deep breath for me. Can you tell me what happened?"

Leif obeyed; Arthur's clothes were soaked and stained with blood all over, but the clear sources were his left arm and his right thigh. They pressed a towel into Arthur's right hand and moved it to cover the wound on his leg, and then grabbed another cloth and clamped their hand over his bicep. He groaned but held still.

"G-Goddamned *vampire*," Arthur hissed through gritted teeth. "I—"

The examination room doors banged open, and Marcus Beldon stormed in. "What happened?"

"It— Father, I'm sorry," Arthur gasped. "It was too fast."

"No," Marcus said coldly as he approached his son. "*You* were too slow."

Leif flicked a glare at him, then quickly schooled their expression.

"Left bicep, right thigh?" Adriyen confirmed, coming to Arthur's side. "Stab or slice?"

Leif panicked for a second when they thought she was asking them; they hadn't *looked* at the wounds, only done as she'd said and covered them. But when they looked up at her again, they found her attention solely pinned upon Arthur. It was as if Leif and Marcus weren't there at all.

"S-Stab to my leg, slice to my arm," Arthur said.

"Okay." Adriyen pulled on a pair of white gloves. "Leif, light some lamps, please, and then bring me a bowl of water and a clean towel. The blue bowl on the shelf above the sink will suffice."

Leif hurried to do as she said, bringing three oil lamps closer to Adriyen's workspace. They set the full bowl and a couple of towels on the small table at her side.

Adriyen instructed Arthur to hold the towel on his arm, and then slowly lifted the one on his thigh. Fresh blood gushed out, and she quickly applied more pressure. Arthur groaned again, his breaths coming quick and shallow. Sweat glistened on his pale skin, mixing with the tears that leaked from his eyes.

Leif went around the table so they weren't in Adriyen's way, and gently touched Arthur's hand. He glanced at them, and they gave a short nod. "You're going to be okay. Squeeze my hand if you need to."

Arthur nodded, screwing his eyes shut as Adriyen released the pressure on his leg. She tossed the soiled cloth to the floor and then used a soaked towel to clear away the blood. Deftly, she slid her fingers beneath the torn fabric of his trousers, then grabbed a pair of scissors from the table and cut the tear wider. She passed the towel over his skin again, then nodded in apparent satisfaction.

"I can stitch both of these with no problem, but this one is fairly deep, so it will take longer to heal than the cut on your arm. Pressure," she instructed Leif, and then went to a cabinet across the room. She returned with a set of surgical tools that Leif didn't have the stomach to look at for more than a second.

"How long until he's back on his feet?" Marcus asked.

Adriyen's gaze was sharp when she glanced up at him. "At least three weeks, especially for his leg. The muscle needs time to heal, even if the surface closes up quickly. Arthur, you'll likely have lingering pain in this leg for several months, but nothing that should hinder your movement or your work. Just be conscious of it, and don't overwork yourself."

She turned to Leif. "Can you get him something to numb the pain while I work?"

Leif nodded and started to leave, but Marcus barked, "No."

Adriyen raised her eyebrows. Arthur cast a wary glance at his father.

"A swig of liquor, if you must, but he can handle a bit of pain." Marcus stood back from the table and regarded Arthur with that icy, uncaring expression. "Every action *and* inaction in a fight has consequences. As I said before: you were too slow, and this is the result. Bear the consequences. To be a Beldon is to know pain, boy, so either get used to it, or be stronger so that this does not happen again."

Arthur stared at Marcus with horror. He flicked a glance at Adriyen at the same moment Leif did, awaiting her response. Her face had gone as stone-cold as Marcus's.

"Master Beldon," she finally said, "with all due respect, I strongly advise against proceeding without pain management. To do otherwise would be, in my professional opinion, negligent and needlessly harmful."

Leif took a small step toward the double doors; surely Marcus couldn't deny that logic.

"I appreciate your opinion, Doctor," Marcus said, every word as sharp as knives, "but I insist you do as I say."

"Do I get a say in this?" Arthur exclaimed. He

tried to sit up but faltered, catching himself on his uninjured arm.

"No," Marcus snapped. "Doctor, see that his injuries are fixed. Arthur, I expect you back to work with sword in hand no more than a week from now." He turned his back on his son and stalked toward the doors. "Clearly, we have a lot of work to do."

Leif clenched their hands at their sides, biting their tongue as Marcus strode by them and through the doors. When they clattered shut, Arthur let out a sob.

Adriyen, however, was silent as death. For several long heartbeats, she stood perfectly still, cold and stony as a statue. Her face betrayed nothing, but Leif could sense her rage.

"Leif," she finally said in a hollow voice. "Go into the cabinet behind me and get the small brown bottle on the top shelf."

They obeyed, moving on soundless feet. They found the bottle and brought it to Adriyen, but she shook her head. Leif understood, then; they set the bottle on the table next to Arthur.

He glanced between Leif and Adriyen, eyes narrowed.

Adriyen stared at him until he reached for the bottle. He grimaced when he uncorked it, and with one final confirming glance at Adriyen, he held it beneath his nose and inhaled.

After about ten seconds, Adriyen blinked once. Arthur set the bottle down.

Twenty seconds later, he fell unconscious on the table.

Adriyen moved as if she'd suddenly woken up from a trance. Leif could do no more than stay out of her way while she worked; the next minutes passed in a blur of hurried movements as she cleaned, stitched, and dressed Arthur's wounds.

When she had finished and discarded her gloves and the bloody towels, Leif helped her remove Arthur's ruined clothes and dress him in a clean, white linen gown. Adriyen checked his pulse, then with Leif's help, carried him on a stretcher into the recovery room. She settled him in one of the beds and placed a blanket over him, then quietly ushered Leif out of the room.

The examination room doors had hardly shut behind them when Adriyen slumped to the floor and let out a sob.

# 10

FOR A MINUTE, all Leif could do was stare at Adriyen. They couldn't reconcile the stony, proud, snappish doctor they'd come to know with the trembling woman beside them now. Adriyen buried her face in her hands and gasped out sob after sob while shudders wracked her body. Her choked sounds lodged between Leif's ribs and pricked their heart like thorns; before they could think better of it, they sank to their knees beside her and placed a hand on her shoulder.

"I-It's all right," they said, but cringed at themself for saying something so hollow. How were they supposed to comfort her? What was the right thing to say to someone who had been vying for their expulsion from this place only a short time ago? Should they try at all, or did she deserve nothing more than Leif walking away?

*No one in this place is your friend.*

But they were here to help *everyone*. Even her.

Leif lightly squeezed Adriyen's shoulder. She sniffed and rubbed her eyes, then pressed her fingertips to her forehead. She didn't look at them, but Leif didn't need her to. Rather, they often found it easier to talk when people *weren't* looking at them. "That was impressive, what you did for Arthur."

She scoffed. "I did my job."

"Exactly," Leif said. "And you did a *good* job." They lowered their voice. "Despite Master Beldon's insistence of the opposite."

Adriyen glanced at them, then ran her hands through her hair and let her head fall back against the door. Her face was flushed from crying, her eyes red around the edges. Stray curls framed her cheeks. "I can't believe he would say that. That he would order me to let his son suffer. I... I didn't think it would be like this, when I took this job. I didn't know he was like that."

"Neither did I," Leif murmured, though they weren't particularly surprised. They thought again of Natasha's bruised face and grimaced.

"I mean, what the hell am I supposed to do?" Adriyen lifted her hands and then let them fall onto her lap. "I've studied medicine for my entire life. When I was in school, I wrote report after report after report on best practices and ethics, and I took an oath to *heal*. To do the least amount of harm. To *care* for people, no matter who they are or how they ended up in front of me. Too many physicians and surgeons look at other human beings and see them as puzzles to be taken apart, specimens to be dissected like the fish and frogs we practiced on. I vowed never to sink that low."

She took a shaky breath and closed her eyes.

"These kids aren't weapons, Leif. They're *children*, for gods' sakes."

Leif gave her a moment, to see if she'd continue. When she didn't, they spoke softly. "You're a good physician."

"Marcus Beldon doesn't want a physician," Adriyen whispered. "He wants a butcher who happens to know how to sew."

"And can you imagine how much worse these kids would have it if that's what he had, instead of you?" Leif met Adriyen's eyes when she turned her head. "You said it yourself: you took an oath to heal. You have a duty—to your own morals, and to these children. Screw what Master Beldon wants; he shouldn't have hired a doctor if he didn't want someone to care for his children."

Adriyen eyed them a moment longer, then let her head fall back again and gazed up at the ceiling. "It's ironic, you know. I've worked here for four years, and in all that time, I've had this...this itch at the back of my mind that makes me second-guess everything. What if I'm not cut out for this like I thought I was? What if my success in school means nothing compared to the actual real-life challenges of this job? What if I'm not good enough?" She breathed a humorless chuckle and shook her head. "And all along, I didn't need to be good at this at all. I just needed to be able to keep them alive, and who cares if they're in pain? Certainly not their father."

"Adriyen." Leif waited for her to look at them again. "You are *more* than good enough. You're exactly what these kids need."

Adriyen blinked a few times and then closed her eyes, exhaling heavily. "You're right," she said softly. "Gods...you're right. I don't know what I was thinking."

"Look..." Leif ran their hand through their hair. "I'm scared, too."

Her eyes flashed open and she sat up straight. "I never said I'm—"

Leif silenced her with a knowing glance. "Who wouldn't be? He's powerful, and he's cruel. He's as unpredictable and cunning as the vampires he hunts. I'd never want to get on his bad side, but that hardly means we have to cower before him. We're both here to help these kids, aren't we? He can't stop us from doing our jobs. You proved that just now."

Adriyen took a deep breath, and then got to her feet. Leif couldn't quite read what was behind her eyes when she looked down at them, but they sensed that something between the two of them had changed. Adriyen no longer glared at them with contempt; Leif dared to wonder if there was almost something like respect in her expression now. Something like understanding.

They felt like they should say something, to acknowledge the fragile truce—if that was truly what hesitated between them now. But they also feared that voicing this sense of understanding would shatter it and return things to how they had been earlier today, when Adriyen had betrayed Leif to Marcus and Leif had been plotting their next petty vengeance. Leif didn't know if they could forgive Adriyen yet, but seeing how she cared for

Arthur in spite of Master Beldon's demands solidified Leif's respect for her. They saw clearly now that, despite their differences, she and Leif had the same goal.

They hoped that she saw that, too.

Leif stood, and before they could decide what to say, Natasha stormed into the office in a whirl of urgency. "Where is he?"

Adriyen straightened. "Mrs.—"

"Tell me what happened, Doctor." She rushed across the room. "Is he okay?"

"He's resting in the recovery room." Adriyen stepped aside to let Natasha into the examination room; she rushed through the doors without hesitation. "He's going to be all right," Adriyen assured her as she followed. The doors swallowed both of them, and Leif was left alone.

Something told them to stay back. Adriyen was there to tell Natasha what had happened and reassure her that Arthur would be okay. Arthur would surely be comforted by his mother's presence. Leif's job, for now, was done.

Or...was it?

Leif waited another minute to see if anyone would come back out, and when no one did, they hurried up to their flat, tea concoctions already brewing in their mind.

Leif returned to Adriyen's office some time later, three cups of tea carefully steadied on a tray. They were relieved to find that neither the door into Adriyen's office nor the double doors into the examination room had latched closed; they nudged through with their shoulder and approached Adriyen, who was hunched over a steel wash basin and vigorously cleaning her tools.

"I brought you some tea," Leif said.

She jerked her head up with a gasp. "Gods, you startled me. Sorry. Um. Thanks. I'll have it in a second."

Leif set the mug down on the counter beside the sink. Adriyen had already returned to her furious washing, oblivious that Leif was still there. Her hands were unsteady as she scrubbed the tools, and her skin was flushed pink from the hot water. Her knuckles and fingertips were scraped raw.

Leif itched to say something, to encourage her to open up, but they knew she wouldn't talk if she didn't want to. They let it go for the moment and ventured into the recovery room. Natasha sat in a chair beside Arthur's bed, and Arthur lay partially propped up on a mountain of pillows. He looked calmer than he had only a short while ago. Leif thought at first that he was asleep, but he opened his eyes and turned his head when they approached.

He smiled. "It's you."

"It's me." Leif set the tea they'd prepared for him on the table beside his bed. "This is an herbal tea that will help your body heal, and stay healthy in the meantime. It'll soothe some of the aches as well. I added a pinch of sugar to mask the bitterness —I hope that's okay."

Arthur nodded. "Thank you, Leif."

"Thank you, Leif," Natasha echoed in a whisper. Her eyes looked glassy, but her smile was genuine.

Leif went around the bed and handed her the final cup from the tray. "This one is for you. I thought something calming would help."

She gratefully accepted it, squeezing their hands as she took the cup.

"Is there anything else I can do?" Leif turned to Arthur.

He shrugged. "I think the rest is up to me. But let's see how long Father actually lets me take it easy." He grimaced. "I know he was serious about going back to training in a week, but I can barely move my leg. I don't know how I'm going to do it."

"You will do no such thing," Natasha said sternly. That fire was back in her eyes again. "You need to heal. I won't let your father throw you back into training until I know you're ready. Leave him to me."

Leif nodded. "All you have to do is focus on resting. Don't worry about anything else."

"How can I not?" Arthur clenched his hands, gripping fistfuls of the knit blanket on his lap. "That was my first proper job since my initial hunt, and I landed myself here. I couldn't even kill a weak vampire without getting myself hurt in the process, and now Father thinks *I'm* weak. If I don't get back out there when he wants me to, he'll only be more disappointed in me. What kind of heir does that make me?"

"Arthur, you mustn't stress over that," Natasha

said, reaching for his hand. "Compared to your health, that hardly matters. Just—"

"It *does* matter," he snapped, snatching his hand back. "*You* don't understand."

Leif steadied themself with a deep breath. There were about a hundred things they could say against Marcus Beldon to assure Arthur that one selfish man's unfair demands did not matter, but the last thing Leif needed was for the Beldon heir to know their grievances with the head of the family. Arthur might not be an adult, but he was Marcus's protégé, and Leif didn't trust that their words wouldn't make it back to Master Beldon.

Besides, they weren't here to turn everyone against Marcus. They were here to be the voice of comfort and kindness.

"You *are* strong," they told Arthur. "You said it yourself that the vampire's actions were unpredictable. Give yourself some grace, Arthur. It was only your second hunt, as you said. You can't expect to have all of your father's expertise immediately."

Arthur's frown didn't ease, but he let the tension out of his shoulders and hands. He slumped back against the pillows with a sigh, and then eyed the tea Leif had brought. Leif grabbed it and carefully placed the cup in his hands.

Arthur took a small sip, and then made a surprised hum as he lowered the cup. "Huh. That's not bad."

Leif smiled. "I hope it helps."

They looked up at Natasha just as her eyes flicked up toward them. Her face smoothed, though a shadow remained over her eyes. She wrapped her hands around the teacup and raised it to her lips, exhaling slowly as she swallowed.

Leif left them both to enjoy their tea. When they passed through the office, Adriyen acknowledged them with a wordless nod. They returned it, then noticed that the cup they'd left her was now empty.

They exited the room with a smile.

# 11

Leif idled in their attic for the rest of the day. While they'd been satisfied with how they'd left the Beldons and Adriyen, as the hours passed their mood plummeted. The events of the day caught up with them—from Adriyen tripping them on the stairs to nearly getting kicked out to Marcus's cruelty toward Arthur—and they found themself cloaked in a cloud of misery.

They curled up on their bed with their heaviest blanket around their shoulders and stared unseeingly at the slice of sky visible out of the little window across from their bed. A neglected cup of tea languished on the bedside table. Whatever comfort or calm that tea could offer was useless to them. They didn't care to relieve the storm roiling in their mind—not this time. What was the point, anyway, when nothing would ever actually get better? They might as well be miserable and stop trying to resist everyone else's efforts to make them so.

They ought to just leave. They should pack up

their supplies and whatever items they could carry, and go somewhere else. No more judgmental aristocrats, no more unreachable expectations. They could leave the city and find a little abandoned cottage on the outskirts of a remote village and become an apothecary for the people there—the only one of their kind, solely responsible for their care. They'd make themself irreplaceable, and then they'd never be kicked out or sent away ever again.

Tears welled in their eyes; they blinked them away. They were sick of crying, sick of losing control of their emotions whenever someone was anything less than pleasant to them. If they were to survive—here or anywhere—they needed to be stronger. They needed to stand up for themself, to fight instead of cower or run away. They knew this; they'd been told this for years. *You crumple like a wet tissue*, their mother had often scolded them. But they didn't know how to control it. They didn't understand how to turn off the flood of emotions.

Maybe their life would be easier if they didn't feel everything so strongly. Was there a tea or tincture for that, they wondered? To numb everything?

They didn't have the energy to pursue that answer tonight, but they could, at least, drink something that would put them to sleep. They were tired of thinking, tired of feeling. They needed to be soundly unconscious.

Leif dragged themself out of bed but kept the blanket around their shoulders as they shuffled across their bedroom and down the steps. They were only absently aware of their actions as they grabbed a tin of tea leaves from the cabinet and stoked a small fire in the woodstove. It took a few minutes, but they realized as they went about the familiar task that they could hear music.

A faint, gentle melody drifted up from the floor below them. Leif recognized Natasha's playing at once, and it gave them pause. The fire poker clattered to the floor. Absently, they shut the grate on the stove and then slumped back on their heels. Their eyes slid shut, and then all they knew was the piano's song, wrapped around them like the soft blanket on their shoulders. Natasha's music was beautiful yet mournful, a lament bleeding out of the keys. It brought tears to Leif's eyes, and finally, they let them fall.

They'd bailed on tea with Natasha tonight, and now they felt awful about it. They hoped she wasn't upset with them. They didn't want to give her another reason to worry about them; while they were happy to accept her kindness, they didn't want to draw too much attention. Natasha had her own children to take care of, *actual* children who needed their mother more than Leif, who was three years shy of twenty and desperately wished they'd start acting like it.

But they couldn't help the affection they felt for Natasha. She'd been kind to them when no one else was, and she'd said it herself that she saw them like one of her children. Would she truly have told them that if she didn't mean it?

She'd forgive them for shunning her tonight. Besides, it wasn't as if she could have done anything differently to defend them today. When it came to Marcus and his decisions, her hands were tied. It was abundantly clear that House Beldon was his and *only* his; Natasha was not his equal.

It occurred to Leif, then, that she just might need a friend as much as they did. Maybe that was why they had connected with her so quickly; they saw their own loneliness in her.

They would apologize tomorrow. For now, they savored the piano's soft lament and hoped that, somehow, Natasha knew they were listening.

Leif hadn't intended to fall asleep on the floor, and they had no idea how long they'd lain there, curled up in a ball beneath their blanket, but when they woke from a disturbing dream to a cold, dark attic, it took them a minute to remember why they were on the floor.

Shivering, they got up and wrapped the blanket tighter as they trudged back up to their bedroom. They nestled beneath their three blankets and hugged a pillow, stuffing their face into it as they waited for sleep to reclaim them.

It didn't.

For what felt like hours, they tossed and turned, trying everything they could think of to make themself relax: counting backwards from one hundred, telling themself a story, burning lavender incense, journaling until their eyes drooped. Each time they started to doze off, their thoughts took off at a sprint, and they found themself staring at the ceiling once again. Their shoulder still hurt from their fall down the stairs, hindering their ability to lay comfortably on their side, and sleeping on the floor hadn't done them any favors.

They rolled over again, winced at the dull throb through their shoulder, and then finally threw off the blankets yet again and got out of bed. Lying there and wallowing in their restlessness was useless; if they were up, then they were up, and they might as well do something productive.

Leif grabbed a thick cardigan from the chair next to their bed, then tromped down the stairs from the loft and stepped into their slippers before heading out of the attic. The fourth-floor hallway was dim and quiet, and Leif padded soundlessly toward the balcony doors at the far end of the hall. Pulling their sweater tighter, they unlatched the paned doors and stepped out into the night.

The sprawling Beldon estate was calm beneath the clear sky. Leif shivered a little in the wintry chill, but the air was still and the cold invigorated them. They sat cross-legged in the middle of the balcony, placed their hands on their knees, and tipped their head back.

*Start with a deep breath.* Crisp air filled their lungs, expanding their chest. They pulled themself up perfectly straight and let their eyes slide out of focus as they exhaled. Bright, endless stars blurred in their vision. White, violet, and indigo mixed and swirled—pure, true chaos. Leif took another deep breath and held it until the little white dots in their vision blended with the stars overhead.

Then, as they finally exhaled, they could read the sky.

Leif had never known why or how they were able to do this. What had started years ago as a means of calming their anxiety and bringing themself out of panic attacks had become a legitimate asset to their work. They'd asked their mother about it once, and she'd told them that until they could read something useful up there, it might as well have been their imagination. Leif still didn't know what she would've considered *useful*, but they hadn't spoken of it again. For five years now, this had been their secret. A personal, private communion with the universe.

They were pretty sure it wasn't their imagination, nor an effect of holding their breath a few moments too long. The stars showed things to them: shapes, shadows, gentle pushes toward one thing or another. Leif had trained themself to quiet their mind of any analysis or assumptions that might've jumped up in response to what they saw; the picture was never complete, the message never clear, until they released themself from this reverie and thoroughly reflected upon what they had seen.

The world seemed so calm when they sat with the sky. Though they watched the chaos of the cosmos swirl above them, it had a strange, ironic order to it. Leif was part of a larger body, breathing and beating in steady rhythm with every single living thing on this planet. That didn't feel chaotic. It felt *right*. It felt...transcendent.

Shadows crept across the sky tonight, a great sweep of dark that threatened to infect and obscure everything else. Leif couldn't find the source of it, but its gnarled claws spread wide and snagged every bright swirl of light. They watched the colors bleed and blend until all they saw was crimson, silver, and black.

A sudden frigid breeze jolted Leif out of their meditation, and suddenly they couldn't stop shivering. They hugged their arms around themself and now stared at the sky with horror. They had never seen anything like that. The omens they received were never so blatant.

Something awful was coming, and Leif couldn't fathom what it might be.

Darkness that ate up everything bright and alive... How literal was this warning? What was the scale of the danger? Did this portend a city-wide disaster, or merely something in Leif's life that was about to go wrong? How scared should they be, and moreover: should they tell someone?

But who would believe them? Natasha? She knew Leif as only an apothecary; if they ran to her now and told her they'd seen a disturbing omen in the stars, she'd tell them they were dreaming. Anyone else would call them crazy.

But if they kept this to themself, and then something horrible happened and people got hurt, Leif would have no one to blame but themself.

They turned and dashed back into the house. They were already halfway to the stairs by the time the balcony doors clattered loudly in their wake. They flung themself down the steps, two or three at a time, and skidded around the corner before sprinting down the hallway toward Natasha's parlor. They stumbled as they halted at the door, and it was only because they grabbed the doorframe to stop their momentum that they saw the door was slightly ajar.

Leif knocked softly, waited a second, then pushed the door open. The room was silent but for Leif's thundering pulse. The utter darkness was stifling, and it all felt *wrong* in a way Leif couldn't articulate. They managed only two more steps into the room before a nauseating wave of dread hit them with enough ferocity to make them dizzy. They blinked rapidly, but in such absolute darkness, all they could see were blurs of colors behind their eyes like persistent sun-spots.

They couldn't get the vision of that creeping darkness out of their mind.

Leif stumbled to the piano by the covered windows and fumbled around until they found a candle. Their shaking hands nearly made them drop the matches, but they managed to catch the flame on the wick, and finally the darkness retreated.

They saw, then, that they weren't alone in the room.

Natasha slouched in her usual chair by the fireplace, hands limp and head lolled to the side. Her lips were slightly parted and her face was calm; she didn't so much as twitch when Leif took a step closer to her. An empty teacup and her ever-present journal sat neatly on the table beside her.

"Natasha?" Leif gently touched her arm, not wishing to startle her awake. "Sorry, it's me. I...I have to tell you something. I'm afraid something's wrong."

She didn't wake. Leif touched her shoulder instead and shook her a little. "Natasha?"

Now their heart pitched with alarm; even a heavy sleeper would be somewhat responsive, if unconsciously. Leif shook her harder, and she finally moved her head—only for it to roll forward listlessly, chin to chest.

Leif gripped both of her shoulders. A white haze of panic encroached upon the edges of their vision; their heart was beating so fast that it hurt. They lifted one trembling hand to Natasha's mouth and counted one,

Two,

Three,

Four,

Five thundering heartbeats.

And felt nothing. Not the scarcest hint of a breath.

Hurriedly, Leif pressed their fingers to the side of her neck and prayed. *Please.*

Seconds passed.

*No. Please.*

Too many seconds.

"Natasha..." The name fell from Leif's lips in a soundless whisper, but their next breath came out in a scream. They seized her shoulders and shook her again and again, sure they must be mistaken. She had to be okay. This was just— just a bad dream. It must be. In a second they'd wake up, and Natasha would be fine. She had to be. *She had to be.*

"What's going on?"

Leif bolted to their feet and faced the door. Poppy Beldon filled the threshold with her lanky silhouette.

Suddenly all of Leif's panic fled. They took a step toward Poppy, placing themself between the girl and her mother. "Poppy," they said, surprising themself with their own steady voice. "Please go get Dr. Adriyen. Your mother..." Here they faltered, but only for a second. "Your mother is ill and needs a doctor. Can you do that?"

"What?" Poppy's eyes widened. "What's wrong with Mom? Tell me what happened!" She started to take a step into the room, but Leif blocked her way. She wasn't much shorter than them, but they drew themself up as tall as possible.

"I don't know what happened," they said calmly. "I just know that your mother needs help, and I need you to go get that help." They swallowed, pleading with her as they met her ice-blue eyes. "Please, Poppy."

She hesitated, then finally nodded and took off down the hall.

Leif shut the door; the moment it latched, their strength left them. They slumped back against the polished wood and let out a single, near-hysterical sob. They couldn't tear their eyes away from Natasha's unmoving form, slouched in her chair as if merely sleeping.

Leif still wasn't wholly convinced she *wasn't*. Maybe she'd taken some kind of sleeping draught that slowed her pulse and breathing so much that it was hardly detectable. Maybe Leif hadn't waited long enough to feel her heartbeat. Maybe she was just comatose. Any explanation would make more sense than the glaring reality that Leif could not accept.

They dragged themself up and went to her again, taking one of her hands only to instantly drop it at the shockingly cold touch of her skin. They swallowed another cry and sank to the floor at her feet, grasping her hand in both of theirs as if they could put the warmth of life back into it. Leif pressed their cheek to her cool, stiff palm and prayed to the stars that she was at peace.

The minutes passed in still silence, and then the door crashed open. "Leif? What happened?"

They raised their head and looked up at Adriyen, letting their tear-streaked face speak for them.

Adriyen's eyes widened. "What..." She bolted into the room, flinging the door shut behind her. Poppy caught it, hot on her heels, but Adriyen spun around and jabbed a finger at the door. "No. Wait outside. Do not argue."

Poppy obeyed without protest.

Adriyen whirled on Leif, and for the first time since they'd met her, they saw real, raw panic in her eyes. She approached Natasha with halted movements, as if getting too close would make true what neither of them wanted to believe.

"Check her pulse," Adriyen said, placing her palm beneath Natasha's nose. "She's not breathing. Do you know what happened?"

"No," Leif whispered. They still held tight to Natasha's hand. "She..."

"Poppy said you told her she was sick. If she declined this rapidly—"

"No," Leif cut in. "I lied to her. She's a child. I couldn't..."

Adriyen met their eyes. "You already checked her pulse...didn't you?"

Leif nodded.

"And she's..."

Fresh tears spilled down Leif's cheeks. They couldn't say it. Their voice fled, and all they could do was look at Adriyen helplessly.

Adriyen bit her lip and touched Natasha's neck, only to instantly recoil. "Oh, gods. Oh...gods." She gently lifted Natasha's right hand and pressed her fingers to her wrist. Her face grew more grim with each passing second until she finally lowered Natasha's arm. She touched her thumb to Natasha's forehead and traced a four-point symbol on her skin, then stepped back and let out a single, quiet sob.

For a minute, neither of them moved. Then Adriyen let out a shaky breath and wiped the tears off her face. "Fuck. Okay. Any idea what... How?"

Leif shook their head, feeling like they were only half present in the room. The other half of them drifted somewhere else, into a different reality where this wasn't happening.

Adriyen turned her attention to the table beside Natasha's chair and picked up the teacup. She tilted it toward the light, then carefully sniffed it. Whatever it was, she recognized it immediately; her face blanched with horror. She thrust the cup at Leif. "Smell this."

They did, then reeled back at the sharp tang. "Wait, but that's... That smells like..."

"Belladonna berries," Adriyen confirmed quietly.

Leif couldn't make sense of this. "She was *poisoned?*"

Adriyen set the cup down and grabbed Natasha's journal next, but no sooner had she picked it up than a page slipped free.

Leif snatched it and angled it toward the scarce light. Their blood ran cold at the very first line, and it only got worse from there.

*If you are reading this, you are too late. You failed, I won, and I'm gone. You remain to wallow in your misery and hate, and I am free.*

*I am finally free.*

*And as you read this, I hope it hits you—I hope it pierces you like one of your precious silver blades—that it is because of you that I'm gone. It is because of you that I could not stand to live another day. It is because of you and your cruelty and your rage and your utterly rotten heart that my only choice was to leave* everything—even my children, who will now all grow up without a mother's love—because *you* were too selfish and proud and cruel.

Well, Master Beldon, I hope you're proud now. And I hope you're miserable. Because despite your best efforts, I no longer am.

I'm free.

A strangled sob broke out of Leif. They dropped the paper and pressed their hands over their mouth.

"What is it?" Adriyen fetched the note, but her tone suggested she already knew what she was going to find. The room was deathly silent as she read.

"Gods," she muttered when she'd finished. The page fell from her hand and settled in Natasha's lap.

"*Fuck*," Adriyen whispered again, and sat down heavily on the coffee table. She met Leif's eyes, then glanced at Natasha, and then slumped forward and put her head in her hands.

Leif didn't know what to do. Their chest ached, as if they'd been stabbed through the heart. Everything else was numb.

They didn't know how long the two of them sat there before the parlor door burst open once again, and Marcus Beldon strode into the room. When his gaze fell upon Natasha, he halted, let the door fall shut behind him, and then approached the chair that held his wife's lifeless body.

Adriyen handed him the note without looking up. "Belladonna berries."

Leif watched Marcus's expression darken as he read, until at last he flung the page to the floor. His hands balled into fists, and just when Leif thought they saw true grief on his face, it morphed into rage.

"Listen to me very carefully." Marcus went to the fireplace, moving with a predator's steady grace. He took a silver dagger from the mantel and pricked the pad of his thumb on its point. His cold eyes found Adriyen, and then Leif. "What you found here tonight shall not leave this room. My wife was attacked by a vampire, turned against her will, and I was left with only one choice."

Quicker than Leif could blink, Marcus thrust the dagger into Natasha's chest. It broke through muscle and bone and drove straight to her heart with a sickening *crack*.

Leif was on their feet before they knew what they were doing. "No! How could you—"

"Leif, stop." Adriyen grabbed their arm, but they wrenched free and threw themself at Natasha, shielding her body with their own.

"*Move*," Marcus growled. "Allow me to finish my job."

Leif sobbed. "Isn't it enough that you killed her once?"

Marcus seized them by the collar of their cardigan and hauled them off of Natasha, and then the strike came so quickly that Leif didn't feel its sting until they found themself on the floor.

Trembling violently, they pressed their palms to the rug and waited for their vision to stop swimming. They were vaguely aware of Adriyen kneeling beside them, but if she spoke they did not hear.

It was Marcus's voice that broke through the ringing in Leif's ears. "Are we quite understood? You will both lose more than your jobs should you speak a word beyond what I have permitted you to say. Is that clear?"

Adriyen's hand tightened on Leif's shoulder. "Yes, sir."

Marcus's sharp gaze bore into Leif. "Well?"

They swallowed a sob, along with every venomous word they wished to spit at this vile man. "Yes, sir."

"Good. Now go. I will deal with the children."

Leif couldn't move. Their body felt like it was trapped in ice, frozen solid and beyond their control. They were hazily aware of Adriyen gently pulling them to their feet; it was only her steady strength at their side that kept them upright.

They looked at Natasha one more time before Adriyen ushered them into the hall.

# 12

THE NEXT DAYS passed in a senseless blur. Leif's world narrowed to the walls of their loft, from which they descended only to eat when the effects of neglecting to do so became unbearable. They assumed that there had been some kind of funeral for Natasha. They assumed that all of her children now knew that she was gone. They assumed that life was starting to crawl forward in House Beldon.

But to Leif, everything had ground to a stop.

Adriyen had tried to coax them out of the attic once, maybe a day or two ago, but Leif had refused to let her in. They didn't know how long she'd stayed out in the stairwell after offering a number of uncharacteristic kindnesses that Leif had turned down, but she had not tried since. Leif almost wanted her to, even if they couldn't fathom the idea of doing anything normal. It seemed wrong to even have a conversation if it wasn't about Natasha. How were any of them expected to just move on? Leif dreaded to know what this house felt like without her.

A faint knock drew them out of their thoughts. It was too close to be from the attic door; it must be someone in the stairwell. But it wasn't Adriyen; when she'd visited, she'd announced her presence with two short, confident raps on the door. This was more like a nervous patter, and Leif could think of only one person it might be.

They climbed out of bed, stumbling as their stiff legs protested the sudden movement, and hurried down from the loft. When they opened the door, they found the youngest Beldon on the other side.

Cyrus clutched a green knit blanket in his little hands and gazed up at Leif with wide, teary eyes. They stepped aside without hesitation and beckoned for him to come in; he eyed them nervously, then took three small steps into their flat.

Leif shut the door softly and knelt on the floor beside Cyrus. "Hey there."

Cyrus's lip wobbled. He murmured something that Leif couldn't understand, and then flung his arms around their neck.

Leif froze in surprise, but quickly recovered themself and held the boy tightly. They remembered how Natasha used to run her fingers through his hair, and gently stroked their hand over his curls. He nestled his head against the crook of their neck, thoroughly affixing himself to Leif.

He cried, but not loudly. Soft whimpers shook his body, and Leif felt his warm tears on the side of their neck. They murmured comforts to him that sounded hollow even to their own ears, but after a while, he calmed. Leif continued lightly rubbing his back and stroking his hair until, eventually, they thought he'd fallen asleep.

Leif took the opportunity to stand up, relieving their numb legs from being folded under them. Cyrus stirred in their arms as they carried him into the kitchen, and seeing that he was awake, they set him on the countertop. "Wait here a moment, okay? I'm going to make us some tea. Would you like that?"

Cyrus wrinkled his nose. "I don't like tea."

"No? Why not?"

"It's like drinking dirt."

Leif chuckled. "It's too bitter for you, then? If I make it sweeter, do you think that'll be better?"

Cyrus shrugged.

"Let's try it." Leif stoked the fire in the stove and set the kettle to boil. They fetched the tin of tea leaves and showed it to Cyrus. "This is chamomile. It makes you calm when you feel restless. Do you ever feel like your thoughts are going too fast?"

Cyrus thought about it, then nodded.

Leif had been hoping he'd say no, but they sympathized. They'd been dealing with anxiety for most of their life, too, long before they knew what to call it. "Whenever you feel like that, you can come up here to see me, and I'll make this tea for you." Leif grabbed the ceramic teapot that Natasha had bought for them. Their heart clenched at the memory, but they pushed the sorrow away and instead let themself feel a swell of gratitude. They channeled the feeling toward their memories of Natasha, hoping that her spirit, wherever it now was, would feel it.

"Your mama bought this for me," they told Cyrus as they set the teapot on the counter. "I saw it in a shop and pointed it out to her, saying that this is my favorite shade of green. I didn't see her buy it, but when we got home, she gave it to me."

They blinked tears out of their eyes and turned their attention back to the tea when the kettle started to rattle. They filled the teapot with water and then dropped a pinch of leaves into it. "Now we give it about ten minutes, and our tea will be ready."

"Why isn't it ready now?" Cyrus asked.

"It has to steep," Leif said. "See how I put the tea leaves in there?" They brought the pot closer to him and lifted the lid. "The leaves sit in the water and the flavors seep out of them until the water becomes tea. When that's done, I'll add some milk and sugar, and then I think you'll like it."

Cyrus nodded once, a very serious expression on his round face. He held up the green blanket that lay in his lap. "Mama made this for me."

"She did?" Leif smiled. "Was it a birthday present?"

"I think so." He hugged it to his chest. "I've had it forever. But...Poppy said I shouldn't carry it around. She said only babies do that."

"Well, I don't think that's true," Leif said. "It's comforting to you. There's nothing wrong with that."

"Really?"

"Really." Leif set their hand on his shoulder. "If it makes you happy, and makes you feel safe, then no one ought to tell you that you can't have it.

Besides, it's a piece of your mother that you can still keep close, even though she's gone now."

Cyrus looked away, turning his head down. "I miss her."

"I know." Leif swallowed thickly. "I miss her, too. But can I tell you a secret?"

Cyrus tilted his head to the side and eyed Leif curiously.

"People who leave us are never completely gone," Leif told him. "You can't see her, and you can't talk to her, and that is...that is really hard. It hurts. But your mother is here in other ways, and sometimes, if we focus carefully, we can feel her presence."

Cyrus frowned. "But she's *not* here. I don't understand."

Leif pursed their lips, unsure how to explain the way their senses picked up on certain presences. They couldn't often achieve a connection to the other side of the veil; it truly did take careful, focused meditation, but on certain nights when the veil was thin, they had seen things they couldn't otherwise explain.

"Do you ever have dreams that feel really real?" they asked Cyrus.

He nodded. "Yeah, but they're scary."

"They can be, yes," Leif said. "But sometimes they're nice, right? And you're a little disappointed when you wake up and realize you were dreaming?"

"Yeah..."

"There are times, in those kinds of vivid dreams, when we can see the people we've lost," Leif said. "Your mama loved you a lot, Cyrus. I think she'll find a way to visit you when she knows you need her."

Cyrus blinked a few times, releasing fresh tears down his cheeks. He took a few unsteady breaths. "But I need her *now*. Why did she go, Leif?"

Leif was too choked up to respond, even if they'd had a good answer. They brought Cyrus into a hug and held him tight. "I don't know," they finally said, struggling to keep their voice steady. "I don't know, Cyrus. I study the universe and I listen to the stars and I try to understand, but there are some things that are just...inexplicable. The universe has no reason—it's just chaos. And sometimes that means we lose people we love, long before we should."

*And too often*, Leif thought bitterly, *the ones who die too soon are the ones who least deserve it.*

Cyrus's arms tightened around Leif's neck. "Mama loved you, Leif. She told me she did."

Leif shut their eyes, releasing a fresh spill of tears. "I know. I loved her, too."

A quiet sniffle, followed by a cough, drew Leif's attention across the room. Adriyen stood at the door, halfway over the threshold as if hesitant to come in too far. She flinched a little when she realized Leif had seen her; they let go of Cyrus and waved for her to come in.

Adriyen blinked, then came across the room. Leif watched her eyes bounce around the simple furnishings before she stepped into the kitchen area. She stopped a couple feet away from them and leaned her hip against the counter, folding her arms across her chest.

She looked tired. The skin beneath her eyes was dark, bruise-like, and her hair was falling out of its bun. Instead of her pressed uniform or prim town clothes, she wore a loose-fitting white blouse tucked into soft trousers. What was especially different, though, was that she'd left the collar of her shirt unbuttoned; it fell open around her collarbones, exposing her neck in a way Leif rarely saw anyone do.

"Sorry to intrude," Adriyen said softly. "I came up to see if you needed anything, and I heard you talking. It was nice, what you said to him."

"Leif makes me feel better," Cyrus said, and smiled for the first time since Natasha had died.

Leif flickered a wobbly smile in return, then busied themself with pouring tea for themself and Cyrus before it over-steeped. They stirred sugar into their cup and both sugar and milk into Cyrus's, then looked up at Adriyen. "Would you like some chamomile tea?"

"I...um..." She toyed with the pendant around her neck. "I'm not really a tea person."

"Says you and literally everyone else in this house." Leif smirked. "Try it. It might make you feel better, too." They fetched another cup and filled it.

Adriyen eyed the tea incredulously when Leif passed it to her, but she indulged them and took a sip. Leif considered it a victory when she didn't immediately look disgusted. "Hm." She tried another sip. "That's actually quite good."

Leif grinned and looked at Cyrus. "What do you think?"

He licked his lips. "I like it!"

"See?" Leif wrapped their hands around their own teacup and took a long sip, savoring the subtle flavor as they swallowed. Already they felt calmer, less fragile, and they knew it was primarily thanks to Cyrus and Adriyen's presence. They chided themself for wallowing in misery these past days when they knew perfectly well how to take care of themself. They had these remedies for a reason, yet too often they neglected their own needs.

They vowed to be better about that, now. If for no one else, then for Natasha, who had cared for Leif more than anyone previously had. And in her absence, the least Leif could do was remember to prioritize their own needs.

Cyrus poked their arm. "Miss Leif? Oh, wait..." He narrowed his eyes, apparently thinking very hard. "Them Leif," he declared, and held up his teacup. "Can I have more?"

Adriyen snorted. Leif couldn't help chuckling as they took Cyrus's cup. "Of course you can. But please, you can just call me Leif."

"I dunno," Adriyen said, "I think he nailed it with 'Them Leif.'"

"It's better than the alternatives, I guess," Leif admitted, pouring a fresh cup of tea for Cyrus.

"I...don't think I ever apologized for calling you 'space girl' before," Adriyen said quietly. "I'm sorry. I didn't know you weren't a girl, but it still wasn't nice."

Leif shrugged. It *had* bothered them, but now, none of that nonsense from their first months here mattered. "Thanks, but don't worry about it. Water under the bridge." They handed Cyrus his tea, though they'd be surprised if he managed to stay awake long enough to finish it; his eyes looked heavy.

"He's getting tired," Adriyen said.

Cyrus, of course, sprang up at that. "I am not!"

"It's okay," Leif told him. "The tea makes you a little sleepy."

"It might be time for a nap, kid," Adriyen said. "I'll take you back to your room."

"No!" Cyrus pouted. "I wanna stay here."

"You can come back anytime you'd like," Leif said, touching his shoulder. Cyrus hugged them again, just as Leif suspected he would, and they used the opportunity to lift him off the counter.

He saw through their scheme immediately and started to struggle, but they'd seen that coming and held fast. "I wanna stay!" he whined. "I wanna stay with you!"

Leif looked at Adriyen cluelessly. "Um...if it'll make things easier, he *can*."

"Are you sure?" She grimaced. "He's not technically your responsibility. Marcus hired a governess."

Leif threw her a doubtful look. "I don't mind. Clearly he wants to be around someone familiar. And...I'd rather not be alone."

"Fair enough." Adriyen tucked a stray curl behind her ear and looked away. "Would...Would it be okay if I stayed for a bit, too? Maybe just...to finish the tea?" She glanced at them, then away again. "Or— Actually, forget it. That was a stupid question. You probably don't—"

"Adriyen," Leif cut her off. "Of course you can stay."

She blinked at them. "What?"

"If you don't want to be alone, you can stay." Leif set Cyrus down and he climbed onto the couch, curling up against one of the pillows. Leif draped a blanket over him and then approached Adriyen. "I didn't realize until today that isolating myself up here was only making me feel worse. I should have welcomed your attempts to visit me before, and I'm sorry I didn't. So please, stay, and forgive me for ignoring you."

"Forgive *you*?" Adriyen shook her head. "Leif, I was so awful to you. If anyone should be begging forgiveness right now, it's me."

"That doesn't matter now," they said. "I do forgive you. I hope you can forgive me for all the rest, too."

Adriyen's eyes turned glassy. "I'm so sorry, Leif."

"I am, too." They lightly touched her arm. "Thank you for being here. And...thank you for being there the other night, too."

Adriyen winced and folded her arms tightly across her chest. "I still can't believe..."

"I know." Leif glanced again at Cyrus; sure enough, he'd fallen asleep with his head resting on the arm of the couch. They nodded toward the door, and the two of them went out into the stairwell. Leif softly shut the door and sat down on the floor in front of it. Adriyen joined them.

"I had no idea," she whispered. "I knew she was often unhappy, and it doesn't take a genius to see that her relationship with Marcus was... troublesome. But I had no idea the extent of it. I can't help but think that if I'd known..."

Leif hugged their knees to their chest. "Yeah. I've been asking myself the same thing."

Adriyen dragged her hands through her hair, tugging out what was left of her bun. Her ginger curls spilled around her face, tangled and uncharacteristically unkempt. "I'd overheard him shouting at her before, but that's all. I never knew he physically hurt her."

"I fear we hardly know the half of it," Leif whispered. "It's never a one-time incident with men like him."

"No," Adriyen agreed, "and her note was proof enough of that." She sighed, shaking her head. "Do you know what the worst part is? No one would believe us, even if he hadn't forbidden us from telling the truth. I don't even think the note would be enough to truly prove how rotten he is. Too many people idolize him, believing him to be the epitome of honorable, polite society."

She was right. The truth of Natasha's death contrasted so harshly with the city's perception of Marcus Beldon that spreading such a 'rumor' would only land them in trouble—with Marcus himself, and with their entire society.

Leif grumbled and set their chin on top of their knees. "I don't know what to do, Adriyen. I'm scared for the kids, and honestly, I'm scared for us. What if he throws us out, because we know the truth? He could ruin both of us with very little effort."

"He won't," Adriyen said, but Leif didn't miss the hint of uncertainty beneath her words. "We'd have more reason to betray him if he got rid of us. He'll keep us here so he can keep an eye on us, if nothing else."

Leif scoffed. "So we're just as trapped as the kids." They shook their head. "I should go now, while I still can."

Adriyen turned to them. "Go where? You said it yourself that you have nowhere else. Leif. Look at me."

They did. "Are you really going to tell me I shouldn't get the hell out of here? You should, too, you know. Both of us deserve better than this place."

"This isn't about us, Leif," Adriyen said. "It's like you said to me after Arthur got hurt: Who do those kids have, if not us? A cruel, withdrawn father who wishes to raise them to be weapons? They need more than that, Leif. Now more than ever, they need someone who will listen to them and care for them. I think we can agree that they will not find that in Marcus."

Leif bit their lip. They didn't have a refute to that.

"We have so little control here," Adriyen went on. "That much is true. But we can do this. We can be here for those kids. That's our job, and I don't know about you, but I feel like I owe it to Natasha to give them the love they won't get from anyone else."

Leif closed their eyes and nodded. "You're right. You're absolutely right. I'm just..." They looked up at her. "I'm afraid that anything we do won't be enough. We can't replace what they lost."

"No, we can't," Adriyen said. "But that doesn't mean we don't have our roles." She reached over and took Leif's hand. "Cyrus came to you today because he needed comfort, and you were the first person he thought of. That means something. You've made an impact on him, and I'm certain you could do the same for Poppy, Joel, and Arthur."

Leif shrugged. "I..." *I just make tea and talk to them. How is that impactful? How is that anywhere near enough?* Doubts gnawed at them, but those voices in their mind sounded terribly like their mother, and Leif knew they were more than that. If Adriyen, who had loathed Leif for the first two months they'd known each other, could see their worth, then they had no excuse to not believe her.

"Thank you," they murmured, squeezing her hand. "I needed to hear that."

She squeezed their hand in return, then let go and stood up. "No one's forcing you to stay, but don't give up. There are people here who need you. And...if you're willing to put the past behind us, I'd like to know you *without* any resentment between us."

Leif smiled. "I'd like that, too."

"Leif!" Cyrus's voice called from the other side of the door.

Adriyen smirked. "You volunteered. I'll see you later." She headed down the stairs, and Leif dragged themself off the floor. They watched Adriyen disappear, and when the lower door had shut, they went back into their flat and returned to Cyrus.

# 13

*Four Weeks Later*

LEIF'S first venture into town without Natasha was bittersweet, but it felt tremendously good to get out of the house and get away from its oppressive energy. They took their time walking to the market, and perused the vendors as if they had all the time in the world. Fresh snow overnight and an overcast sky kept most people indoors this morning, but Leif wasn't deterred; they would rather shop without a pressing crowd around them anyway.

They bought the herbs they'd come here for, and then treated themself to a cup of hot chocolate and a pastry from the baker's stand before making their way back to the Beldon estate. They sipped the hot drink as they put away the herbs and crushed some leaves for a poultice, and the familiar task would have been relaxing—even enjoyable—if not for their hair constantly getting in their face. Every few minutes they had to pause to push it behind their ears, and it refused to stay. The shorter pieces that framed their face were especially irritating, and Leif had half a mind to do something drastic involving the washroom mirror and a pair of scissors.

But that gave them a better idea.

They finished the poultice and bottled it, then put everything away and grabbed their sewing scissors from the box next to the couch. Then they left the attic and went down to the first floor, knocking softly on Adriyen's office door as they poked their head in.

"Can I ask you for a favor?"

She looked up from the papers she had spread over her desk. "Oh, hi. Sure, what do you need?"

Leif held up the scissors. "I know this isn't exactly your expertise, but will you cut my hair? It's getting too long and it's bothering me. I'd do it myself, but I'm sure I'd butcher it."

"I'm honored that you believe I'll do any better," Adriyen said. "I can try, but certainly not with those tiny scissors. Let me see what I have." She went to one of the cabinets by the door to the examination room.

Leif was a little nervous that she'd return with some deadly-looking surgical tool, but she turned around with a perfectly normal set of scissors that had longer, narrower blades than the little ones Leif used to trim threads.

Adriyen gestured toward her desk chair with a

flourish. "Have a seat. Hopefully you don't hate me—or your haircut—when I'm done."

"Honestly, if you screw it up, it gives me a reason to shear it all off," Leif said as they sat down. They'd never worn their hair shorter than shoulder-length, partly because their mother had always talked them out of cutting it, insisting that it would look terrible, but also partly because Leif had never felt courageous enough to make such a drastic change.

"How short do you want it?" Adriyen asked.

Leif shrugged. "Just take off a couple of inches, I guess. Enough to get it out of my eyes and clean up the ends."

Adriyen was quiet for a minute. "How short do you *actually* want it?"

Leif turned their head to look at her and found a sly smile on her face. Their heart gave a nervous flutter; could they really just...do whatever they wanted? No one was here to stop them, no one would judge them, and the only person likely to talk them out of it was themself. For the first time in their life, they had absolute freedom with their appearance.

So why shouldn't they start making themself look how they wanted to look?

"Chop it," they said to Adriyen. "All of it. As short as you possibly can without taking a razor to it."

She grinned. "That's what I thought. Ready?"

Leif nodded and turned their head forward. They held their breath when Adriyen lifted up the length of their hair.

"One...two...three!" With a few quick snips, the first several inches fluttered to the floor. Leif let out a giddy giggle, already feeling a weight off their shoulders. There was no going back now—no changing their mind. Their confidence grew with every snip of the scissors, and they buzzed with anticipation as Adriyen worked. They resisted the urge to ask her how it looked each time she stepped in front of them to see how she'd done.

"Almost there," she declared at last, making a few final snips before she stepped back. "I mean... I'm no barber, but it could be worse. C'mere, there's a mirror in the other room."

She led them through the double doors and into a small washroom, but stopped in their path before they could fully enter the room. "Actually, wait. Close your eyes."

Leif did, biting back a grin. They heard the soft *tink* of an oil lamp igniting, and saw the soft glow through their eyelids. Adriyen's hand gently touched their arm, guiding them forward a few steps.

"Okay. Open!"

Leif blinked as their eyes adjusted to the light, and for half a second they did not recognize themself. But their reflection's eyes widened when theirs did, and staggered closer to the sink basin when they did, and raised their hand in unison with Leif as they touched their hair in utter disbelief.

*That's me*, they thought in amazement. *Stars above, that's really me.*

It looked *perfect*. Sure, it was a little uneven, but it fell in a way that made it look natural, as if it was always meant to be styled this way. It curled a little around their ears and stayed in place when they pushed it back off their forehead. They shook their head and mussed it, running their hands through it over and over, amazed at how different it felt.

"So...I think this means you like it?" Adriyen grinned at them in the mirror.

Leif spun around, and without a second thought, threw their arms around her.

"Oh!" Adriyen let out a surprised chuckle.

"*Thank you*," Leif breathed, and then let go. They couldn't resist turning to the mirror again, and it struck them that they'd never admired their appearance like this before. Nothing about how they looked had ever felt this *right* before. "I...I can't believe that's me."

Adriyen smiled. "You've wanted this for a long time, huh?"

Leif nodded. "I really did. But I didn't think I was brave enough."

"Huh, that's exactly what I thought when I applied to the academy of medicine." Adriyen's smile turned wistful. "And you know what my mother told me?"

Leif met her eyes in the mirror. "What?"

"Do it scared." Adriyen leaned against the doorframe. "She told me that bravery wasn't about *not* being scared. It's about doing things in spite of the fear and knowing you're strong enough to handle the outcome." She tilted her head to the side. "You know, Leif, you're pretty goddamned brave."

"Me?" They turned around. "What, for cutting my hair?"

"No. For being here. For *staying* here."

They blinked at her. It didn't feel like bravery, to remain in this house and this job that they had not chosen. In many ways, it felt like defeat. It felt like letting their mother win by doing exactly what she wanted them to do without defiance. Yes, House Beldon had terrified them—and still did— but they hadn't even tried to resist their fate. They could have gone anywhere that day their mother kicked them out, and yet they trudged here and followed her plan.

And as for staying, well...they hadn't really had a choice. Where else would they have gone? How else would they have survived? They wanted to think they would have figured it out, but they couldn't be sure.

"You don't believe me." Adriyen spoke gently, but the words still made Leif wince.

"N-No," they stammered, "I mean...if I was brave, I would've stood up to my mother when she kicked me out. I would have taken my life into my own hands instead of coming here. And even if I had still come here, there's a thousand ways I could have defended myself and even Natasha and then maybe..." They sighed. "I don't know. Maybe if I wasn't so scared, if I had said something or done something..."

"Oh...Leif." Adriyen touched their shoulder. "It's not your fault."

They knew that. And yet.

Adriyen was quiet for a minute. "If you have time, there's something I want to show you."

Leif eyed her curiously. "What is it?"

Adriyen gestured toward the double doors. "Come outside with me."

That didn't answer Leif's question, but they followed her anyway. They went out of the infirmary and she led them out through the sunroom at the south end of the house, across the garden, and down the hill toward the tree line. It was only then that Leif realized where she was taking them.

"What's out here?" Their voice betrayed the trepidation they felt at approaching the old stone tower hidden among the trees surrounding the estate.

Adriyen spared them only a brief glance over her shoulder. "Something I think you should see."

# 14

LEIF FOLLOWED Adriyen in silence for the rest of their walk. The tower rose up before them as soon as they stepped beneath the shade of the trees, a crumbling cylinder surrounded by tangled rosebushes. Leif eyed the thorny thicket warily, but Adriyen strode confidently toward the bushes. When Leif trailed after her, they found a well-hidden break in the branches that formed a narrow path up to the tower.

"What is this place?" they asked as Adriyen threw her shoulder against a weathered wooden door. It protested loudly, but eventually opened with a rusty screech.

"The last remnant of a castle that used to stand here." Adriyen stepped into the dark maw that yawned before them now. "It's centuries old, and I guess the only reason the Beldons left it alone when they built their mansion is because Julius Beldon—the family's founder—had a strong interest in ancient history. Maybe he thought he'd find something valuable in here, I dunno."

Leif hesitantly followed her into the dark. Even with daylight spilling in through the door, the shadows were suffocating. A thick odor of rot filled the air and slicked the back of Leif's throat. Worse, however, was the dark sense of dread that doused Leif like a frigid rain. They hugged their arms around their body as they shuffled across the dirt floor, trailing Adriyen toward a set of stone steps that spiraled endlessly up.

"I'm surprised this thing is still standing," Leif muttered. If there had been a proper floor at any point, it had long rotted away. Spider webs clung to every corner, and Leif could hear mice scuttling around. The stone walls dripped with moisture that pooled in shallow puddles across the floor. Stones had crumbled or fallen loose in some places, leaving holes in the walls that pulled pale sunlight through.

"Me too," Adriyen admitted.

Leif turned toward her and caught her looking at them strangely. "What?"

She quickly glanced away and started up the stairs. "Nothing. Come on, we're going up."

Leif tipped their head back and eyed the spiraling stairs. "All the way up?"

"Yup." Adriyen's voice echoed off the walls.

"Right." Leif took a deep breath to settle their nerves before they followed Adriyen. It wasn't the height that bothered them, but that dreadful weight that both beckoned them closer and warned them away.

The two of them climbed in silence. Leif became conscious of the rapid patter of their heartbeat as the stairs took them up and up; they had to consciously remember to breathe normally so as not to succumb to the panic that frayed their nerves. Something was so *wrong* about this place. They dreaded what they might find up at the top.

"A-Adriyen?" Leif hated how small and desperate their voice sounded in the still air, but they couldn't stand the heavy silence any longer. The darkness was deafening and tricky; Leif was starting to fear, irrationally, that Adriyen wasn't ahead of them at all. "Tell me what we're going to find up there."

She didn't reply. Leif's heart pitched with certainty that their fears were true, but then Adriyen spoke. "Trust me, it's easier to show you. But...I think it will clarify some things about Natasha."

Leif winced. They'd thought as much, but they'd wanted to be wrong.

*Why here?* they wondered. *What brought you up here?*

After what felt like an eternity, they reached the end. The stairs brought them to a small landing at the very top of the tower. A single door stood before them, and Adriyen approached it without hesitation. It opened easily, and Adriyen disappeared into the room.

Each step that Leif took forward felt like dragging their feet through molasses. They realized they were shaking; their stomach was in knots, their skin was covered in gooseflesh. This room seemed to bare its teeth at them, warning them away. Yet the oppressive force wasn't violent or dangerous; it was...frightened.

Leif paused before the threshold and closed their eyes. They took a long, steady breath in and held it. *You don't have to be frightened. I am here as a friend. Please don't be afraid. Your secrets are safe.*

They waited a few moments, and ever so slightly, the room's energy changed. Leif's pulse settled, and the coil of dread in their stomach eased. When they stepped forward into the dim room, they almost felt welcomed.

Adriyen stood opposite the door, facing the small window positioned high on the stone wall. Pale light drifted in, casting the space in a ghostly pallor. The air was still and stale and carried a faint, familiar scent of cinnamon that hit Leif like a strike to the face.

Leif needed only a quick glance around the room to put the pieces together. The room was cluttered and lived-in, furnished with mismatched pieces that had seen far better days, but everything clearly had its place and its purpose. A small standing piano was pushed up against the wall beneath the window, its keys left uncovered as if the last person to play it had stepped away for only a moment. A faded sofa faced a tall, crammed bookcase, and a heap of knit blankets took up one end of the sofa. An unfinished one lay draped across the arm, still trailing a ball of yarn. In the corner, two easels leaned against the wall, one bearing a half-finished painting whose canvas had collected a thick layer of dust. A jar of brushes and a basket of paints sat atop a stack of unused canvases on the floor.

Leif took it all in and felt like their heart was

fracturing all over again. This space was so purely *Natasha*, so untouched by everything *Beldon*, that to see it after her death was like looking at a shrine. A frozen moment of life, stilled, never to proceed forward.

Adriyen reverently touched the piano keys, brushing her fingers over them without pressing hard enough to make a sound. When she turned to Leif, her face was streaked with tears. "I don't know what compelled me to come up here, but I was— I went up to the graveyard the other day, and on my way back to the house something drew me here. I swore, it was like..." She looked away and clenched her jaw. "It sounds crazy, but it was like she was calling me here."

"No, that's not crazy," Leif whispered.

"It hurt, seeing all of this," Adriyen continued. Her eyes were glassy as she gazed around the room. "She kept so much of her life hidden away up here. I hate that she felt like she *couldn't* be herself in that house. I hate that that fucking monster drove her to hide up here."

Leif nodded, too choked up to reply. They wandered over to the bookcase and traced their fingers lightly along the weathered spines. The books looked old, many of them with creased spines and loose binding. Each row was packed from end to end, with additional books tucked on their sides across the tops of the others. Many of them appeared to be novels, but the bottom row was entirely books on painting and drawing, and Leif spotted well-worn journals scattered throughout the volumes.

Their heart stuttered. They were tempted to reach for one, to read Natasha's musings as if that were a way to hear her voice one last time. But they feared they'd find fresh misery in her writings, and they did not wish to break her trust.

"Here." Adriyen approached Leif with a similar journal in her hands—the one Natasha had left on the table the night she'd died. "I took it with me that night. I didn't want to leave it with...him." She smoothed her thumb across the cover. "It belongs here with the rest of her."

"And...the note?" Leif's voice came out as a rasp.

"It's in there. I hid it in the back." Adriyen blinked fresh tears out of her eyes. "Maybe someday we'll be able to talk about it. Maybe there will come a day when the truth has to be told."

Leif placed their hands over Adriyen's so they held the journal together. "I hope so."

Adriyen met their eyes and nodded, then let go. Leif squeezed the book tighter, then fanned the pages as they turned to the shelf. They didn't mean to read it, just to catch a glimpse of Natasha's handwriting—a last glimpse of her. A page slipped free and Leif snatched it, heart lurching as they remembered the horror they'd felt reading the note she'd left. They could barely stand to look at it now. Quickly, they folded it and tucked it back into the journal.

"Wait," Adriyen said. "What was that?"

"Huh?" Leif frowned. "Her note. You just said—"

"No, it wasn't." Adriyen took the journal from

Leif's hands and opened it to the random page where they'd stuck the loose paper. "I put her note in the very back, tucked into a pocket on the last page. This one fell out of the middle."

"It's probably just..." But Leif trailed off when Adriyen unfolded the page and they saw, unmistakably, their own name at the top.

Oh, gods.

Adriyen blinked a few times and then offered the page to Leif. "It's...for you."

Leif's hand trembled as they took the paper. Their heart ached at the sight of Natasha's handwriting, and for a moment the words blurred before their eyes. *Good,* they thought hazily, *this room doesn't want me to read this.* And then the tears spilled down their cheeks, and everything came back into focus.

My dear Leif,

By the time you read this, I will be gone. I hope you can forgive me.

I don't know what will happen next, and I don't know if I will find the peace I desperately want to find. I feel like I am failing you— you, and my children—in the worst way a mother possibly can. This guilt will choke me even in death, so if you are angry and if you hate me, know that even if I am at peace, I will always have this knowledge that I betrayed you.

I'm sorry.

You brought light and kindness and love into my life in a way that few people have ever been able to do. I treasured every moment I spent with you, my dear, and I regret that I don't have the strength to carry on. Please do not think this is because you did not do enough.

If there's one true lesson I have learned from the hunters and their blood-soaked lives, it is this: You can't save everyone. That doesn't mean you shouldn't try, but sometimes, you lose —the monster wins—and all you can do is try again.

Keep trying, Leif. It was too late for me, but I leave you with those whom I treasured most: Arthur, Poppy, Joel, and my dear little Cyrus. I know you will be there for them with your gentle presence and your comforting words, and this gives me hope for them. I am grateful you are there.

Leif paused there as a surge of anger rose up within them. How *dare* she? How could she do that? How could she soundly admit her guilt and the unfairness of it all and then still go through with it? Couldn't she be grateful for Leif's presence while also staying alive?

Hot, heavy tears spilled from their eyes. They hastily wiped them away and kept reading.

Even still, I know, this isn't fair to you—or to them. I wish it didn't have to be this way. I wish I wasn't writing this. But I don't know what else to do.

I've been fighting to survive just one more hour, just one more day, just one more week—and on and on and on— for years. I can't do it anymore.

Once again, I'm sorry.

I hope that the brief time we spent together was as special to you as it was to me.

Take care of yourself, Leif. You

*deserve every kindness this world has to offer.*

*Natasha*

Leif was fully crying by the time they reached the end. They gripped the page in both hands and read those last lines over and over until their tears blotted out their vision. They were only vaguely aware of Adriyen gently guiding them to the sofa, and the faint scent of cinnamon and cranberries that clung to the blankets only made them cry harder.

Yet even as their shoulders shook with each heavy sob, they felt a strange warmth in their chest. It was Adriyen's hand on their shoulder, they knew, but they swore they felt another presence too. That warmth spread through them like summer sun sinking into their skin, and they knew that Natasha was here.

*I forgive you*, they told her. *I'm so sorry.*

The warm feeling intensified briefly, and then faded.

Leif dried their tears and blinked at Adriyen. They took a deep breath. "Thank you."

"For?" Her voice was thick with emotion.

"Bringing me up here." Leif folded Natasha's note and tucked it into their pocket. "You're right, it's wrong that she had to hide these parts of herself, but it's also comforting to know that she held onto all of this despite her suffering. She carved out a safe space full of the things she loved instead of just giving them up. I needed to see that."

Adriyen's eyes were distant as she nodded. Leif could tell that her thoughts were miles away. "Do you..." She trailed off, and it was a minute before she spoke again. "Are you still thinking about leaving?"

"No." They didn't know what their days here would bring, but their resolve had hardened in the weeks since Natasha's death. They refused to leave those kids.

Leif turned their head to look at Adriyen. "Are you?"

She shook her head. "Not anymore." Her eyes found theirs. "I think we'll need to have each other's backs, though, if things get...tricky."

"Can I trust you to do that?" Leif asked. They wanted to, but part of them was still wounded from how Adriyen had treated them before.

"You can." Adriyen held their gaze. "I swear it to you."

Leif nodded once. They didn't expect the two of them to be without their disagreements, but they'd be a fool to deny that things had changed. Adriyen deserved a second chance.

"Then you can trust me to do the same," Leif told her. "I'll support you however I can, but if you go, I go."

"And if I stay," Adriyen said, "you stay. Deal?"

"Deal." Leif flickered a smile that quickly fell when they glanced up at the crowded bookcase. "We should agree on a threshold, though. A point of no return, in case things get worse."

They weren't sure how things could get worse than they already were, but that omen in the stars still painted their dreams in crimson, silver, and black. They had assumed that Natasha's death was the disaster the stars had spoken of, but now they weren't so sure. Was that event, horrible as it was, just the catalyst of a much more catastrophic series of problems?

"I think we'll know," Adriyen said, "when it's time to go."

Leif dearly hoped it never got to that point, but they couldn't let their guard down. Now more than ever, they needed to pay attention to the messages in the world around them. They might not be able to change anything, but at least they could be prepared.

And, come what may, they would not have to weather it alone.

# AUTHOR'S NOTE

Thank you for reading *The Solace of Stars*. This story took me by surprise in many ways; I knew that Leif—who appears in my novel *Silver Blood* as a side character—demanded their own tale, but the way this story unfolded was quite unexpected. In particular, I did not expect it to delve into such heavy topics. But mental health is important to talk about, even when it's hard.

If you or someone you care about is struggling with mental health or going through a hard time, know that there are resources out there to help:

National Suicide & Crisis Hotline: 988
National Domestic Violence Hotline: (800) 799-7233
Trans Lifeline: 877-565-8860
The Trevor Project: 866-488-7386

You are not alone. You are loved. It can get better. Please stay.

# ACKNOWLEDGMENTS

One thing about me is that I love quirky side characters, and another thing about me is that I can't resist constructing elaborate backstories for said side characters. So is anyone surprised that what started as a short story, once again, ended up as a novella?

Still, this book wouldn't have made it to the finish line without help from some marvelous people. Firstly, I must thank my partner for requesting—nay, *demanding*—more Leif content. I might've already had a few ideas brewing, but it's thanks to all our late-night brainstorming that this story came together. Thank you for always cheering me on, bouncing ideas when I get stuck, and endlessly supporting me. 🤍

Endless gratitude to Tabitha for being a brilliant beta reader, as always, and helping me dig into the core of this story to make it stronger. I appreciate your insight more than I can say.

Many, many thanks to S. Jean for the absolutely stunning cover of the paperback edition. You brought my vision to life spectacularly!

As always, thank you to my readers. I would keep writing books regardless of whether people read them, but it's still pretty damn cool when they do. So if you're reading this right now, *thank you*.

# ALSO BY T. L. MORGAN

CITY OF SILVER

*Silver Blood*

*Sweet Sorrow*

FADED MOON

**PUBLISHED AS TALLI L. MORGAN**

THE WINDERMERE TALES

*MELIORA*

*TRANSCENDENCE: AN ANTHOLOGY OF CHANGE*

# ABOUT THE AUTHOR

T. L. Morgan, who also publishes as Talli L. Morgan, writes fantasy books for adults and young adults. When they're not writing, Talli enjoys drawing, playing D&D, and thinking about writing. You are also likely to catch them in the library as they go about their day as a professional question-answerer.

You can learn more about Talli's books on their website, tallimorgan.com.

 instagram.com/tallimorgan.books

 bsky.app/profile/tallimorgan.bsky.social

www.ingramcontent.com/pod-product-compliance
Lightning Source LLC
Chambersburg PA
CBHW031517010826

48973CB00013B/2640